bangkok noir

bangkok
noir

John Burdett	Stephen Leather
Pico Iyer	Colin Cotterill
Christopher G. Moore	Tew Bunnag
Timothy Hallinan	Alex Kerr
Dean Barrett	Vasit Dejkunjorn
Eric Stone	Collin Piprell

Edited by Christopher G. Moore

Heaven Lake Press

Distributed in Thailand by:
Asia Document Bureau Ltd.
P.O. Box 1029
Nana Post Office
Bangkok 10112 Thailand
Fax: (662) 260-4578
www.heavenlakepress.com
email: editorial@heavenlakepress.com

First published in Thailand in 2011
by Heaven Lake Press
Printed in Thailand

Jacket design: K. Jiamsomboon

ISBN 978-616-7503-04-2

Contents

Introduction *vii*

Gone East by John Burdett *1*

Inspector Zhang and the Dead Thai Gangster
by Stephen Leather *23*

Thousand and One Nights by Pico Iyer *75*

Halfhead by Colin Cotterill *91*

Dolphins Inc. by Christopher G. Moore *117*

The Mistress Wants Her Freedom
by Tew Bunnag *151*

Hansum Man by Timothy Hallinan *175*

Daylight by Alex Kerr *203*

Death of a Legend by Dean Barrett *219*

The Sword by Vasit Dejkunjorn *239*

The Lunch That Got Away by Eric Stone *255*

Hot Enough to Kill by Collin Piprell *277*

Introduction

Behind the Thai smile and the gracefully executed *wai*, in the near distance is another realm: the geography of conflict, personal grudges, anger, revenge, disappearances and violence. Where loss of face, personal rivalry and competition for power often have fatal consequences. The risk of danger, like an irregular heartbeat, is unpredictable. Most of the time the danger is out of sight, out of mind. But when it unexpectedly explodes, the victim goes down hard and doesn't get up.

Glide along the daylight surface of Bangkok, and the gritty world of noir often seems light years away. The surface is polite, pleasurable and fun— *sanuk*. But dig deeper below the *sanuk* layer, and the tropical paradise reveals a far colder, damp darkness of lost souls—souls stranded, battered and estranged. Writers are often among the first to kick over that noir rock, and their readers watch as the spiders, scorpions and cockroaches scatter in all directions.

The dozen authors in *Bangkok Noir* lever their collective boot to that stone in the heart of the City of Angels. Hints of noir appear like blimps on the Bangkok radar screen. The members of local charities who cruise around in vans to collect the dead and injured are called body snatchers. Newspapers announce the latest official crackdowns, which in the past have been directed at bar closing hours, abortion clinics, car thieves, hired gunmen, speeders and underground lotteries. And whispers posted on the social networks speak of unofficial shakedowns. At every turn there is a new noir-like incident, such as the Bangkok temple morgue, found to contain two thousand aborted fetuses. Art follows such dark spaces of human activity. Already a horror movie about the morgue is in the works for 2011, titled *2002 Baby Ghosts*. Noir in Bangkok happens fast. The subject of noir is often taken from the latest headlines of the *Bangkok Post* or *The Nation*. And of course the noir history of past coups looms, casting a long black shadow that feeds the fear of future coups.

The potential list of subjects is long, but the stories in this collection will give more than a few insights into the Thai noir world. The idea of the national sport, Muay Thai—a combination of ballet, boxing, kicking and kneeing—is pure noir. That's the idea of *sanuk* dipped in bruises and blood. Muay Thai may be closer to assassination than normal boxing. Whatever it is (or isn't), Muay Thai is the sport of noir. With ancient rituals and music the fighters perform before a huge, cigar smoking, game fixing, betting crowd, where gangsters, fraudsters, boiler room operators, bar owners and crooked cops and officials, wearing gold chains and amulets, gather. The kind of men who know each other's birthdays and what's expected in terms of keeping the wheels greased. Men and women with advance knowledge of who is going to win before the fight starts.

There is no consensus on the definition of "noir" that covers all cultures. Writers don't agree on one version of noir, and photographers and painters translate noir into their own image of darkness. Slowly, a general idea of noir in Bangkok has emerged over the last ten years. The foreign and Thai artistic noir movement has been growing during this period. Ralf Tooten, an award-winning photographer, has captured Bangkok noir in his photographs (one of which graces the cover of this book). The artist Chris Coles has painted the faces of men and women who move through the Bangkok underworld. The authors represented in this anthology, foreigners and Thais, have contributed stories that create powerful images, bringing the Bangkok noir movement another step forward. Thais and foreigners live together inside the world of noir. These stories record their experience of Bangkok's dark side.

Bangkok Noir contains twelve short stories by professional authors who have developed an international reputation for their writing about life in Asia. Not all of the writers in this collection are crime writers or even, normally, writers of fiction. What unites them is their knowledge of Bangkok, their depth of cultural understanding and their love of storytelling. As a group they are professional authors whose books are published in many countries and languages. You will find a diversity of original voices and perceptions of noir—as well as various approaches to tone, structure and characterization—in these deeply felt, insightful and thought-provoking tales. This volume is special for another reason: it is the first time that foreign and Thai professional writers have combined their visions of Bangkok within a single volume.

I opened this introduction with a comment about the ambiguity of noir as a concept. It is worth noting some basic background. "Noir" is the French word for black or dark. The French used the term to describe certain dark films portraying characters doomed by the hand of fate. Appropriated years ago by Anglo-Saxon critics and authors, the word "noir" in English has been used to describe a certain category of crime fiction. American authors like Thompson, Willeford, Goodis and Cain made a reputation selling a bleak, nihilistic vision of life. The contemporary notion of noir, traceable to the original French idea, is based on an existential space where the characters find themselves caught without the possibility of redemption. Noir fiction chronicles a world where a person's fate is sealed by a larger and more powerful karma, one from which, despite all efforts, they can't break free. The stories in this collection are in the tradition of past noir authors who were masters at leading characters onto the platform, slipping the noose around their necks and springing open the trap door.

What Westerners call a fatalistic vision of life, in Asia often passes as karma. All of those good and bad deeds from your past life work themselves out in the streets, bars and back alleys of this life, and there's not much room for free will inside this concept of a universe where payback awaits in the next life.

With this anthology this group of authors, known for their writings about Thailand, have put their creative talent to the task of showing that noir is geographically unbounded. If noir is looking a little tired in the West, in Thailand it has all the energy and courage of a kid from upcountry who thinks the Khmer tattoos on his body will stop bullets. Dark stories, like a good *som tum*, need the right number of red hot peppers to press the pain and pleasure buttons, and when a noir writer runs short of hot peppers, he throws in a Thai dame (she may be a ghost), knowing she can drive any man to ruin with the flash of her smile.

What makes Bangkok noir different from, say, American, English or Canadian noir? There's no easy answer. But a stab in the heart of noir darkness suggests that while many Thais embrace the materialistic aspects of modern Western life, the spiritual and sacred side draws upon Thai myth, legends and customs, and remains resistant to the imported mythology structure of the West. In the tension between the show of gold, the Benz, the foreign trips and designer clothes, and the underlying belief system creates an atmosphere that stretches people between opposite poles. I like to think of noir as the by-product of the contradictions and the delusions that condemn people to live without hope of resolving the contradictions. No matter how hard they struggle, they can never break free.

Take a late night walk through some poor neighborhoods in Bangkok. Hear the *soi* dogs howling as the angry ghosts launch themselves through the night, and and observe that modern possessions don't stop the owners from making offerings to such spirits. In the slums life is short and cheap, and it's a tough life filled with uncertainty and doubt. But noir isn't just about the poor or dispossessed. The rich occupy their expensive condos and drive their luxury cars, sheltering inside the circles of influence and power, only they, too, like the poor, can find their world overturned by an accident of fate, stripping them of their safety and exposing them to terror and loss.

No one is going to provide a definition of "noir" that satisfies everyone. Critics and writers try to distinguish hard-boiled fiction from noir fiction. Strip away the fancy stuff and it comes down to nothing more than this: the difference between hard-boiled and noir is the difference between hemorrhoids and cancer. Hard-boiled stories make for uncomfortable reading, but you know somehow there's the possibility of hope at the end (no puns are allowed in noir). Noir is black in the way certain death is black. No redemption, no hope, no light at the end of the tunnel.

Tough guys, players, losers, the tormented and lost souls all appear in *Bangkok Noir*. But the heart of *Bangkok Noir* is the existential doubts that haunt the characters. Many of them are expatriates washed up like pilot whales on the shore, thinking that someone is going to save them. Instead they get rolled over, sliced up and processed as another part of the food chain. The heat, the corruption, the lies and double-crosses, the bars and the short-time hotels conspire to lull, entrap, encircle and finish off anyone who betrays the system.

In Bangkok there is an old trail that leads through a thicket of historical noir cases told by Thai storytellers of the past. Books and TV shows have created a mini-industry around the likes of See Ouey, the Chinese-Thai cannibal executed in the 1950s for murdering half a dozen young children. His preserved body is exhibited like a ghoulish alien creature inside a see-through display case at the Forensic Museum.

Another noir celebrity is the ill-fated Jim Thompson, not the noir writer, but the American (rumored to be a CIA agent) who reintroduced silk-making into Thailand and who mysteriously disappeared on a walk in the Malaysian jungle. His body was never found.

This anthology of contemporary stories weaves a pattern of intrigue and mystery where the living and the dead occupy the same space. Crooked lawyers, crooked cops, transsexuals, minor wives, killers and ghosts take you along for a tour that unlocks the secret doors and invites you to enter into the space where Thais and foreigners work, live, play and die together. The only mystery not uncovered by the writers in this collection is why it has taken so long for a volume of *Bangkok Noir* to appear.

Christopher G. Moore
Bangkok
February, 2011

Gone East

John Burdett

1.

Go East Young Man

Anyone with a brain who followed this advice between, say, the end of WWII and the beginning of the 1990's, is probably a millionaire by now, most will be in the ten million bracket, some are even captains of industry—but who was *giving* such advice? Answer: my Uncle Walter.

I only met him once when I was fourteen: long hair, sandals, beads, a deep fondness for trees and an extreme gentleness that could seem phony— oh, and a big marijuana habit, too. He took me to the Glastonbury music festival for a week and, by means of mystical argument, did his best to liberate my mind from its suburban prison. My mother had always spoken of her brother in ambiguous terms, sometimes as the black sheep of the family, at others, more wistfully, as the only one who found freedom;

she never forgot to mention that he was a polyglot, like all the male members of her family, including me. In his endless travels he picked up languages like shells on a tropical beach. From my point of view it was a momentous meeting: there weren't very many rebels left by the eighties.

Mum warned me not to be overly influenced by Walter, whose profound hope it was that he would die in the shadow of the Himalayas. The mountains granted his wish somewhat earlier than he had anticipated by means of untreated amoebic dysentery at the age of forty-two. His death left me at a forked path: should I follow the fear-based path of respectability, or take my chances with dharma? Or was there a way of hedging my bets?

I inherited his diary and his advice to go East, which I adapted to my own needs: after all, flower power had long been eclipsed by dough by the time I reached my twenties, and Uncle Walter was already pushing up poppies somewhere in the Hindu Kush. Nor did I expect to *stay* East; no, his diaries had seduced me, I had to visit those magic places, which he described with a gigantic literary gift he never exploited—then I was going to go *West*, to make real money.

Yeah, right. In the event I fell in love on my first trip to Bangkok (Thailand was second in Walter's list of favorite places, after Ladakh). My true love's family found me a lawyer who got me permanent residence: it was a lot easier in those days. So I married her, learned the language—everyone was astonished at how quickly I picked it up (I had the weirdest feeling that Walter was helping me out with the tones from beyond the grave) and eventually graduated from one of Bangkok's finest universities with a first class law degree, all financed by my Thai in-laws, who then set me up in a tiny office off Silom and left me in no doubt that it was payback time. They even posted spies: any working hour I spent away from the office, unless on business, was reported to my wife who reported back to me in chiding tones.

And they sent me clients. You need to have practiced law to really have a feel for just how low, dirty, petty, vindictive, fascist, sociopathic, paranoid and sick the fabulously rich really are: every client they sent fit into that category. Oh yes, and there was another unspoken condition attached to the generosity they had shown me: certain cases I had to win, no matter what. Bribing became my principle forensic skill. I've been doing it for so long now, I could do it standing on my head. I can even do it without saying anything: I know all the tea ladies in all the government and corporate departments who are trusted to take brown paper envelops from one office to another, concealed under the dish cloths on their trolleys. There are a lot of wealthy tea ladies in Bangkok.

Now even my enemies say I'm more Thai than the Thais and if, in middle age, I am suffering from the self-disgust that lawyers like me need to feel in order to convince ourselves we're still part of the human family—well, I have two trump cards left to save my soul. One is Uncle Walter—just recently I've taken to reading his diaries again, I even had them copied onto Microsoft Word so I can study them at work without the in-laws suspecting: they still post spies, I'm pretty sure my second secretary is in their pay. My other solace is Om.

Okay, you've guessed that Om is not my wife. True. Neither is she one of the over-paid whores at the over-priced brothel I have to visit every Saturday night with my brother-in-law Niran as part of our family male bonding ritual (it's that or snort cocaine with the middle brother, or get drunk out of my mind with the youngest). Om is my innocence, Om is my soul. She came into my life mysteriously (she drove her trolley into mine at the big delly in the basement of the Paragon: a clear violation of aisle eitquette I thought, and said so in gutter slang; she stuck out her chest and tongue at the same time as putting her thumbs to her temples and wiggling her fingers: it was hilarious).

I don't share Om with anyone. I even take precautions when I visit her in the condo I bought her, which happens to be one block away from my office. I go to her via the supermarket which has two exits onto two different streets… She thinks it's funny the way I always arrive with unnecessary groceries. She loves nature, by the way, especially trees, and is gentle to a fault. I also supply her with marijuana that the cops give me for free: I'm far too good a customer for them to even think of charging. Not that she uses it much. In fact, I'm not sure she ever really wanted it—with her infallible intuition she saw that I needed to smoke a single joint with her as part of our Friday afternoon love-ins, when I shut out the world and everything that has happened to me since I first arrived. And if that's not impressive, let me tell you: her intuition is not limited to minor bad habits: in bed she knew, from the beginning, *exactly* what I needed. Not many men have experienced that level of service, so allow me to report: it's irresistible. Don't look for it unless you want to be an emotional slave for life. Om knows all about Uncle Walter, of course; I had to tell her so she could be included in my secret life. She reads his work as part of her English language studies.

2.

Om comes (she says) from a very small village on the Cambodian border where everyone is tattooed and speaks Khmer as a first language. Her tattoos are in an ancient Khmer script and, I do believe, are faithful reproductions of still more ancient Hindu spells and magical incantations that can be traced back to the Arians and the *Vedas*. When I first slept with her she watched the expression on my face when I found the tattoo on her upper left thigh about two centimeters from the entrance to her vagina. I still have no idea what it says and I don't know why I gulped when I saw it. How can a single syllable in an alien script make anyone gulp? It had an effect though. After the first time I saw it, I became very horny—outrageously so for a man of my age. Since then the tattoos have increased. At the time of writing she owns another at the small of her back, one on her left shoulder and one more about half an inch below her navel. So far as I know they are all ancient Khmer script and represent Bronze Age Brahmin magic.

There's another curious thing about Om: she loves the shrine to Mae Nak not far from On Nut Skytrain station on the Phrakanong canal. I can't remember how many times I've gone there with her. She always buys candles and incense and spends about fifteen minutes in profound meditation whenever she visits. You know the story of Mae Nak of course? That brave and noble Thai wife for whom death was no obstacle: she continued to take great care of her husband and family even as a ghost. For my money Mae Nak deserves the title as patron saint of Bangkok, considering how popular she is; there's always a crowd of women at her shrine when Om and I visit.

Everyone remembers the punch line: one day while the ghost Mae Nak was preparing *nam phrik* in front of her husband on the floor of their wood house, she dropped a lime through a gap in the floor boards. The lime landed in the cellar below and, without a thought, Mae Nak effortlessly extended her arm to a length of twenty feet to retrieve it. Her flesh-and-blood husband saw, realised he'd been living with a ghost and freaked.

Okay, I'm going to make a confession here: on the morning of the day Om and I first made love together Om took me to Mae Nak's shrine and as we were both kneeling she took my left hand and pressed it on her upper left thigh. I wondered what she was doing; then, later that day, when I saw her naked I realised she had pressed my hand on her tattoo. I bought her condo a week later, because I knew even at that stage I could not survive without her.

Now, so far nothing I've related can be said to be totally out of the ordinary; a little eccentric, perhaps, with plenty of Oriental exoticum, but nothing to which you wouldn't lend credence, right? So here's the stretcher: last Friday afternoon when I visited I saw she had been busy redecorating the condo. Well, maybe *redecorating* is an extravagant word for the half hour she must have spent with a felt tip pen and a spray gun. They were everywhere. What were? The *tattoos*, of course. The one on her thigh was reproduced above the front door and again on the bedroom door. The others, those on her back, shoulder and belly, appeared in either black or red at various places all over the flat. Then there were the sculptures: carefully carved and polished pieces of blackwood all about twelve inches in length, all on wrought iron stands, all highly artistic three-dimensional reproductions of the tattoo on her thigh, placed at strategic positions near doors and windows.

Yes, I was taken aback, but not overly so. If she had been practicing black magic on me, I was pretty satisfied with the result so far—I don't want to sound mean spirited, but compared with the sex life I'd had at home for the past decades… So I made no objection and even confessed that simply seeing that single ancient Khmer syllable (whatever it meant) in black over the front door was giving me a hard-on. But the magical inscriptions were only a tiny part of the shock to my sense of reality that day. Instead of taking me straight to the bedroom, as she usually did, Om gave me a special excited smile and showed me where she'd reached in Uncle Walter's diary, which she was reading on her laptop. She had taken the trouble of inserting an electronic book mark, so that as soon as she had started Word, we were taken to a paragraph in Walter's diary which read:-

Spent all day yesterday at Mae Nak's temple at On Nut, right on the Phrakanong canal. I don't know what it is about that myth that grabs me. Hallucinations all night, and I haven't smoked a thing. The sorcery is so strong, the whole stretch by the canal, with the flowers, lotus buds, incense sticks and the statue, radiates power. I know Thai women feel it, however vaguely, that's why there's always such a crowd.

Now, the problem was that such a passage did not appear in Walter's diary, although it is a pretty good imitation of his style. I ought to have known, for at certain times in my life I'd spent whole years reading him, I knew his masterpiece by heart, and *such a passage did not appear in it.* Rather than argue with her, or allow myself to be distracted in any other way from the jolt to the crotch that her redecoration had delivered the moment I entered the flat, I simply shook my head and forced a smile. After all, I had only to return to my office later to check with the hand-written original, which I kept in the safe there.

Om's magic worked even better than usual that day: five times, squeezed into the couple of hours I'd allowed myself for lunch. Naturally, as soon as I'd showered and kissed my amour goodbye, I rushed back to the office to retrieve Walter's script. It is in the form of school exercise books of various gaudy colours, more than one hundred in all. I knew, roughly, the dates when he was in Bangkok, so it was not difficult to find the book, and then the page, which Om had been reading on her laptop. Now the green balls really started to run down my legs: this is what I found in Walter's inimitable spidery script:-

Spent all day yesterday at Mae Nak's temple at On Nut, right on the Phrakanong canal. I don't know what it is about that myth that grabs me. Hallucinations all night, and I haven't smoked a thing. The sorcery is so strong, the whole stretch by the canal, with the flowers, lotus buds, incense sticks and the statue, radiates power. I know Thai women feel it, however vaguely, that's why there's always such a crowd.

A cold sweat broke out all over my body. I knew, for certain, that passage had not been in the original. But I was *looking at* the original, and there it was. No question but that the safe was inviolable: a floor-to-ceiling Chubb with high tech extras, it was ridiculous to think Om or anyone working for her could have broken into it. Anyway, there was no sign the script had been tampered with, and only a counterfeiter of genius could have forged Walter's handwriting and even then how would they have inserted such a paragraph in an old traveler's journal where every last space was used up?

I was scared. Very very scared.

3.

Fear was not my only reaction, however. I was also thrilled, intrigued, fascinated—and it would be coy not to admit to a certain hope that something inexplicable to law and science was happening to me. I was not wrong. No sooner had I put Walter's journal back in the Chubb and locked it, than my first secretary came into my room to say that a new client was waiting to see me. This also was anomalous. All my clients came through my wife's family connections and always made contact with my second secretary, who did nothing except network with my in-laws. My first secretary was trained in law and was brilliant at all she did but could not network to save her life. When I exchanged a glance with her she shrugged and jerked a chin at the waiting area. I nodded. She left the room to return a few seconds later with a tall, slim, wiry Southeast Asian man in his sixties with long gray hair in a pony tail, a wispy gray beard and piercing eyes. I understood immediately that he was a type one comes across from time to time in Asia: somehow, perhaps through some mystic or martial discipline, he had retained an undeniable vigor, as if the virility of youth still empowered his hard body. When I offered him a chair, he shook his head. Instead he came up to the desk, looked down to study me with intense curiosity for a moment, then said in Thai with a thick Khmer accent: "Your wife is dying. Go home now."

I raised my eyes slowly until they looked into his, which were blazing black. While we were mesmerizing each other, I realized he had started to undo the top buttons of his shirt. He continued until he had undone each one all the way down to his waist band. When he pulled his shirt open, I began to understand. His flesh was a mass of black tattoos, amongst which I had no difficulty in discerning those forms and shapes that I had seen earlier that afternoon at Om's condo: the same, of course, as those on her body.

Naturally, I called my driver and rushed out of the office to the pick-up area outside the building. My car was a high-end Lexus with tinted windows; when we reached the walled compound, where my in-laws had built a set of fine detached houses slap bang in the middle of downtown Bangkok, the great gates opened automatically, then closed with a clank behind us. For more than twenty-five years I had loathed that clank, so similar, in my mind, to the clank of prison gates.

As soon as the driver stopped the car I dashed into our house, ignored the maid who stood in the middle of the lounge looking depressed, knocked softly on my wife's bedroom door and waited for her low, soft, pathetic "Come in."

If I've said almost nothing about my wife so far it is for one simple reason: guilt. Lalita—always shortened to Lali—had never done me any harm and I really did love her once: why else would I have made so much effort to please her family? Lali, though, was one of those Asian women who are simply not sensual. We had produced no children and, except for the first months of marriage, hardly made love more than once in a blue moon to convince each other we were still an item. Soon after that Lali lost interest in love making altogether, then, a decade later, in the world. She has spent most of her middle age in her bedroom where childhood friends and her favorite aunt visit her. Whenever we meet we both feel a great sadness that things have worked out this way. I am proud to report that each of us has found the strength not to blame the other: sometimes life simply is like that. The thought, therefore, that I may have inadvertently caused her death by the vilest form of Khmer sorcery through taking Om as a *mia noi*, was dreadful to me beyond words. Believe it or not I began to resolve, at that moment, to drop Om. Passionate as I was about her, I could not countenance, or live with, the murder of Lali by witchcraft.

I was in quite a state, in other words, which was made worse by the doctor who was just leaving. He caught me at the door and said in a tone which I found accusatory: "Massive cancerous growth behind the stomach, too deep to operate…"

"How long does she have?"

"About a week, if that."

I closed—almost slammed—the door behind him and went to Lali who lay on her bed watching me. I pulled up a chair, took her hand, pressed it to my lips and said: "I'm so, so sorry. So very very sorry," and burst into tears.

She caressed my head with her hand. "Don't worry, it's all going to be alright."

"How can you say that?" I said, bawling.

She smiled and said: "If you stop making a noise I'll tell you."

4.

"This is not an easy question for me to ask," Lali said in a weak voice, her head sunk into the pillow, locking eyes with me for a moment, then looking away. "Tell me the truth, have you ever felt that you were set up by me and my family?"

"Set up?" I scratched my jaw.

"Don't lie. It's way too late for that."

I thought about it. "By you, no. You're far too innocent. By your family—maybe, in an opportunistic way. After they got to know me they realised they were going to have the lawyer they always wanted: clever, respected, street wise and, being a *farang*, entirely dependent on them for clients and funding. I have to admit, they were right to think they needed one. If not for me everyone of your male relations would be on death row or serving life sentences."

She took away the hand that had been holding one of mine and her features tensed to such a degree I feared she was going to have a seizure. "You're wrong, I'm afraid. Quite wrong. I am as much a product of these people as my three brothers. How could I not be? I was brainwashed from birth. They sent me out to find a *farang* like you whom they could manipulate, and since I was their zombie, their robot-like all good little upper class gangster girls—I did as I was told. *This is the way the world is*, was their message, *these are the kind of things you have to do to survive.* And: *look at the money we've spent on you, didn't you realise it would be payback time one day? Everyone else is earning their keep.* What did I know? I'd never had an independent thought in my life. If you remember, I even faked an interest in sex at first."

"Lali," I said, "I can't believe you're saying this."

She ignored me. "But when I saw how basically noble you were, and how you had that peculiar British integrity—which my charming family sees as stupidity—that forced you to carry on with what you had started, even if you had a frigid wife and the mob for in-laws, I started to feel terrible. Really terrible. So terrible I could no longer live a normal life. You see, in my own frigid way I had finally fallen in love with you, but being a psychic nonentity I had no libido. I think I might have developed sexually, if I hadn't been so depressed about it all. It's been cowardice and self-disgust that's kept me pinned

15

to this bed—this damned room—all these years. If I'd had one atom of courage I would have told you to pack our bags and take us to the Himalayas—I dreamed of living in a cave with you in a state of total poverty." She sighed. "But I waited too long. Middle age caught up with me. It was too late."

"Lali, you're killing me with this," I said.

She put a hand out for me to hold. "But not to worry, this is Thailand. There is always a way around such things."

I frowned. Whatever could she mean?

She beckoned me to come closer. "The Mae Nak shrine—your uncle Walter's mysticism—they sowed seeds in my mind, but there was nothing I could do until Bunthan came to see me."

"Who?"

"The Khmer man who came to your office today. I sent for him through my Aunt Nit, whose husband is also from Cambodia. Bunthan is a shaman of the old Khmer school that has its roots in ancient Brahmin sorcery." She had to pause for breath. I could see her heroic struggle with weakness and nausea and felt worse than ever. She continued: "He has been teaching and training me for ten years. I wanted to tell you immediately but he wouldn't let me. He reminded me of how fatal weakness and impatience can be—look what misery those faults had brought me already."

"Teaching and training you in what?"

For a long moment she did not answer. Indeed, she seemed already to inhabit a different world. "Advanced techniques in cheating death," she said at last in a whisper.

"But you're dying—the doctor said so?"

"Yes," she said with a grave nod, "but thanks to Bunthan I'm going to cheat. We are going to be saved by ancient magic, my love, working through me. Indeed, you could almost say that in your case you have already been saved. Just promise me one thing—that you'll play the game and won't freak out like Mae Nak's husband?"

"How can I promise anything when I have no idea what you're talking about? I'm sorry, you have to tell me more."

Lali sighed, then beckoned me to come close to her mouth. I could see in her face all the suffering of the decades, and the toll her disease was taking. Her voice shook when she said: "All these years I've spent mostly in bed–immobile, you see, more or less dead."

"So?"

"He showed me how to…"

"How to what?"

She raised her head with great effort to say: "Project the etheric body, also known as the ghost body. It can be done, you know, consciousness can live anywhere, *it can even create its own vehicle.*" Then she collapsed back onto the pillow and closed her eyes.

"No," I said, "you can't leave it at that." I shook her. "You've got to tell me what's going on. What did you do to Uncle Walter's diary?"

She smiled very faintly. "Bunthan said it had to be done that way. It's part of the architecture of your mind that your Uncle Walter has to be on your side. After all, he's the one who brought you to Thailand in the first place, he's your real life guru. You needed at least a hint from him. I read the diary to Bunthan, who is illiterate in everything except ancient Khmer, and even then he can only read magical incantations. He says your Uncle Walter was very advanced, but there was a paragraph missing from the script, which Walter deliberately left out because you weren't ready, but now had to be replaced."

I stared at her with aggressive incomprehension until, with great effort, she pushed me away, then started to drag the sheet off of her. She was wearing a cotton dressing gown, which she pulled up until her pubic hair was exposed. I breathed in sharply: there was that same tattoo about two centimeters from her vagina, identical in every way to the one Om also wore in the same place. I needed no further prodding. I pulled open her dressing gown and made her sit up. Sure enough: the same tattoos as Om in identical positions on her shoulder, belly and lower back.

She was quite exhausted and could hardly manage the last words she ever said to me: "I'm going to make it up to you. What you've seen so far is only the beginning."

She died that same night.

5.

I typed the foregoing notes, Reader, in a state of great agitation the day after Lali died. On reflection they appear to me as a crude attempt at exorcism, and I trust you will forgive a certain hysteria inherent in the account, which is, I can assure you, nevertheless true in every particular. Now, six months have passed and everything has changed.

I waited a decent length of time before moving Om into the compound. The ex-in-laws didn't like it, but there was nothing they could do. They knew something occult was going on, over which they had no control—and in any case, there's no way they can survive without me. Just to be on the safe side, I also moved Bunthan into the compound, because he terrifies them. In other words, Lali's death has made me prince of the fort, a veritable boss or *jao poh*, who runs the show. I am finally free and intend to celebrate by taking Om on an extended vacation to the Himalayas: we'll be spending quite some time in Ladakh. I can't tell you how excited she is.

Life has improved in other ways, too. I'll give an example. Om and I have developed our social life to the point where we've learned to enjoy even the stuffiest side of my profession. When we went to a Law Society dinner last week they sat us more than ten places away from each other on opposite sides of the infinite table. Both of us were stuck with brain-numbing bores on either side, but it didn't bother us at all. Just as the high court judge on my right was starting into an insufferable diatribe against the latest criminal law amendment statute, I felt a friendly tug at my crotch, followed by the unzipping of my pants by petite expert hands and a long, slow, humorous caressing of my member. True, Om was sitting more than thirty feet away, but distance is no problem for one of her reach. Of course, I don't call her *Om* anymore when we're alone. I call her by the name of the master who is projecting her: Lali.

John Burdett

John Burdett was brought up in North London and attended Warwick University where he read English and American Literature. This left him largely unemployable until he re-trained as a barrister and went to work in Hong Kong. He made enough money there to retire early to write novels. To date he has published six novels, including the best selling Bangkok series: *Bangkok 8; Bangkok Tattoo; Bangkok Haunts* and *The Godfather of Kathmandu*.

Inspector Zhang and the Dead Thai Gangster

Stephen Leather

Inspector Zhang looked out through the window at the fields far below. There was so much land, he thought, compared with his own Singapore. The nearly four million population of the island state was crowded into just 253 square miles, and there was little in the way of green space. But Thailand had green in abundance, criss-crossed with roads and dotted with small farms, and in the distance mountains shrouded in mist. He closed his book with a sigh. It would soon be time to land.

"Are you okay, Inspector?" asked Sergeant Lee, removing her headphones. She was twenty-four years old and was wearing her hair long for a change, probably because while they were on the plane, they weren't, strictly speaking, on duty, even though they had been sent to Bangkok by the Singapore Police Force.

"Of course," said Inspector Zhang. "Why would I be otherwise?"

"I don't think you like flying," she said. "You did not eat the meal, you have not availed yourself of the in-flight entertainment system and you seem... distracted."

Inspector Zhang shook his head. "I am fine with flying," he said. "In fact I have a Singapore Airlines frequent flyer card. Two years ago I flew to London with my wife, and the year before that we went to visit relatives of hers in Hong Kong."

"London?" she said. "You went to London?"

"Just for a week," he said. "It was always my dream to visit 221B Baker Street, and to follow the trail of Jack the Ripper."

"Who lives at 221B Baker Street?" asked the Sergeant.

"Why, Sherlock Holmes, of course," said Inspector Zhang. "Though I have to say that it was something of a disappointment to discover that in fact there is no 221B and that the only building that comes close is the home of a bank." He shrugged. "But it was fascinating to see where the evil Ripper plied his trade and to follow in his footsteps."

"He was a serial killer in Victorian London, wasn't he?"

"And never caught," said Inspector Zhang. He sighed. "What I would give to be on a case like that, to pit my wits against an adversary of such evil. Can you imagine the thrill of the chase, Sergeant?"

"I'm just glad that I live in Singapore, where we have one of the lowest crime rates in the world."

"For which we are all thankful, of course," said Inspector Zhang. "But it does tend to make a detective's life somewhat dull." He sighed again. "Still, I have my books."

"What have you been reading, sir?" asked Sergeant Lee.

Inspector Zhang held up the book so that she could see the cover. The title was *The Mysterious Affair at Styles* by Agatha Christie. "It is one of my favourites," he said. "It is the book that introduces the greatest of all detectives, Hercule Poirot. I never tire of reading it."

"But if you've already read it, then you know how it ends," said Sergeant Lee. "There is no mystery."

"The solution is only part of the enjoyment of reading mystery stories," said Inspector Zhang, putting the book into his briefcase. "Agatha Christie wrote thirty novels featuring Poirot, and I have read them all several times."

She frowned. "I thought that Sherlock Holmes was the greatest detective, not Poirot."

"There are those who say that, of course," said Inspector Zhang. "But I would say that Sherlock Holmes relied more on physical evidence, whereas Hercule Poirot more often than not reached his conclusions by astute questioning." He tapped the side of his head. "By using ze little grey cells," he said, in his best Hercule Poirot impression.

The plane shuddered as the landing gear went down.

"Have you ever travelled abroad for work before, Inspector?" asked Sergeant Lee.

"This is the first time," said Inspector Zhang. He had been asked to fly to Thailand to collect a Singaporean businessman who was being extradited on fraud charges. At first the fraudster had fought his extradition, but he had been denied bail, and after two weeks in a crowded Thai prison he had practically begged to go home. He was facing seven years in Changi Prison, and as bad as Changi was, it was a hotel compared with a Thai prison, where thirty men to a cell and an open hole in the floor as a toilet were the norm. Inspector Zhang had been told to take an assistant with him, and he had had no hesitation in choosing Sergeant Lee, though he had felt himself blush a little when he had explained to his wife that the pretty young officer would be accompanying him. Not that there had been any need to blush. Inspector Zhang had been married for thirty years, and in all that time he had never even considered being unfaithful. It simply wasn't in his nature. He had fallen in love with his wife on the day that he'd met her, and if anything he loved her even more now. He had chosen Sergeant Lee because she was one of the most able detectives on the force, albeit one of the youngest.

The plane kissed the runway, and as the air brakes kicked in Inspector Zhang felt his seat belt cutting into his stomach. The jet turned off the runway and began to taxi towards the terminal, a jagged line of wave-like peaks in the distance.

"And this is your first time in Thailand?" asked Sergeant Lee.

"I've been to Thailand with my wife, but we flew straight to Phuket," he said. "I have never been to Bangkok before."

"It is an amazing city," said Sergeant Lee. "And so big. I read on the internet that more than eight million people live there."

"Twice the population of Singapore," said Inspector Zhang. "But the crime rate here is much, much higher than ours. Every year the city has five thousand murders and at least twenty thousand assaults. In Singapore we are lucky if we have two murders in a month."

Sergeant Lee raised a single eyebrow, a trick that the Inspector had never managed to master. "Lucky, Inspector Zhang?"

"Perhaps 'lucky' is not the right word," admitted Inspector Zhang, though if he had been completely honest, the inspector would have had to admit that he would have welcomed the opportunity to make more use of his detective skills. In Singapore unsolved murders were a rarity, but he knew that in Bangkok hundreds went unsolved every year.

The plane came to a halt on the taxiway, and the Captain's voice came over the intercom. "Ladies and gentlemen, I am sorry, but there will be a slight delay before we commence disembarkation," he said. "And in the meantime, would Inspector Zhang of the Singapore Police Force please make himself known to a member of the cabin staff."

"That's you," said Sergeant Lee excitedly.

"Yes, it is," said Inspector Zhang.

Sergeant Lee waved at a stewardess and pointed at Inspector Zhang. "This is him," she said. "Inspector Zhang of the Singapore Police Force. And I am his colleague, Sergeant Lee."

The stewardess bent down to put her lips close to his ear, and Inspector Zhang caught a whiff of jasmine. "Inspector Zhang, the Captain would like a word with you," she said.

"Is there a problem?" he asked.

"The Captain can explain," she said and flashed him a professional smile.

Inspector Zhang looked across at Sergeant Lee. "I think you had better come with me," he said. "It can only be a police matter." He pulled his briefcase out from under the seat in front of him, put his book away and then followed the stewardess down the aisle with Sergeant Lee at his heels. There was a male steward wearing a dark grey suit standing at the curtain, and he held it back for them to go through the galley to the business class section. Three stewardesses were gathered in the galley, whispering to each other. Inspector Zhang could see from their worried faces that something was very wrong.

"What has happened?" Inspector Zhang asked the steward. He was wearing a badge that identified him as the Chief Purser, Stanley Yip.

"The Captain would like to talk to you," said the steward. "He is by the cockpit." He moved a second curtain and motioned for the inspector to go through.

There were thirty seats in the business class section, two seats at each window and a row of two in the middle. A large Indian man wearing a crisp white shirt with black and yellow epaulettes was standing by the toilet at the head of the cabin, talking to a stewardess. He looked up and saw Inspector Zhang and waved for him to join him.

"I am Captain Kumar," said the pilot, holding out his hand. He was at least six inches taller than Inspector Zhang, with muscular forearms and a thick moustache and jet black hair.

Inspector Zhang shook hands with the pilot and introduced himself and his sergeant.

The pilot nodded at the sergeant and then turned back to the inspector. He lowered his voice conspiratorially. "We have a problem, Inspector. A passenger has died." The pilot pointed over at the far side of the cabin, and for the first time Inspector Zhang noticed a figure covered in a blanket huddled against the fuselage. The window's shutter was down.

"Then it is a doctor you need to pronounce death, not an officer of the law," said Inspector Zhang.

"Oh, there's no doubt that he's dead, Inspector. In fact he has been murdered."

"And you are sure it was murder and not simply a heart attack or a stroke? Has he been examined by a doctor?"

"According to the Chief Purser he is definitely dead, and there is a lot of blood from a wound in his chest."

"Who put the blanket over the victim?" asked Inspector Zhang.

"The Chief Purser, Mr. Yip. He thought it best so as not to upset the passengers. He did it before he informed me."

"The body should always be left uncovered at a crime scene," said Inspector Zhang. "Otherwise the scene can be contaminated."

"I think it was probably the first time he had come across a crime scene in the air, but I shall make sure that he knows what to do in future," said the Captain.

"I still don't understand why you need my services," said Inspector Zhang. "We are on Thai soil. This is surely a matter for the Thai police."

"It's not as simple as that, Inspector Zhang," said the Captain. "I have already spoken to my bosses back in Singapore, and they have spoken to the Commissioner of Police, and he would like to talk to you." He handed the Inspector a piece of paper on which had been written a Singapore cell phone number. "He said you were to call him immediately." He waved a hand at the door behind him. "You are welcome to use the toilet if you would like some privacy."

Inspector Zhang looked around the cabin. The four cabin attendants were watching him from the galley, and there were seven passengers sitting in the first-class section, all looking at him. "I think you're right," he said. "Please excuse me." He nodded at Sergeant Lee. "Sergeant, please make sure that no further contamination of the crime scene occurs, and make sure that everyone remains seated." He handed her his briefcase. "And please put this somewhere for me."

"I will, sir," said Sergeant Lee as Inspector Zhang pushed open the door to the toilet and stepped inside. He closed the door behind him and looked around. The room had been recently cleaned and smelt of air freshener.

Inspector Zhang took out his cell phone and slowly tapped out the number that the Captain had given him. The Commissioner answered on the third ring. Inspector Zhang had never spoken to the Commissioner before and had only ever seen him at a distance or on television, but there was no mistaking the man's quiet authority on the other end of the line. "I understand that there is a problem on the plane, Inspector Zhang."

"Yes, sir, there is a body."

"Indeed there is. And from what the Captain has said, it is a case of murder."

"I can't confirm that, sir, as I have not done anything in the way of an investigation. But the pilot tells me that the man is dead and that there is a lot of blood. Sir, we are on Thai soil, and as such any investigation should properly be carried out by the Thai police."

The Commissioner sighed. "I wish that life were as simple as that," he said. "There are a number of issues that require resolving before the case is passed over to the Thais, not the least being that we need to know exactly where the plane was when the murder was committed. If it was in international air space, then it will be a case for us to handle in Singapore. We also need to take into account the nationality of the victim and the perpetrator."

"The perpetrator?" repeated Inspector Zhang. "Are you suggesting that I solve the crime before allowing the Thai police on board?"

"I am told that you do have a talent for solving mysteries, Inspector Zhang. And from what I have heard, it is a mystery that confronts us."

"But we have no forensic team. I am not even sure of the cause of death."

"If a murder has been committed, the one thing we can be sure of is that the murderer is still on the plane. So long as the doors remain closed, the murderer has nowhere to go."

"So I am to conduct an investigation before anyone can leave the plane?"

"Exactly," said the Commissioner.

"But this is a Boeing 777-200, sir. There must be more than two hundred people on board."

"All the more reason to get started, Inspector Zhang. I have already spoken to my opposite number in the Royal Thai Police Force, and he is happy for us to proceed. To be honest, Inspector Zhang, they would be content for you to solve the case and for us to fly the killer home to stand trial in Singapore."

"But if we don't solve the crime, then the plane remains a crime scene and will have to stay in Bangkok for the foreseeable future?"

"Exactly," said the Commissioner. "And nobody wants that. The last thing we want is for the world to believe that our national airline was somehow tainted by what has happened. Inspector Zhang, I am assured that you are the man who can handle this smoothly and efficiently."

"I shall do my best, Commissioner," said Inspector Zhang.

"I am sure you will," said the Commissioner, and he ended the call.

Inspector Zhang put away his cell phone and stared at his reflection as he drew back his shoulders and took a deep breath. He exhaled slowly, then took out a plastic comb and carefully arranged his hair. Then he removed his spectacles and polished them with his handkerchief. He was fifty-four years old and had served the Singapore Police Force for almost thirty of those years, but he could count on the fingers of one hand the true murder investigations that he had been involved with. Most murders, especially in Singapore, were committed by relatives or co-workers, and generally investigations required little in the way of detecting skills. But what he now faced was a true mystery, a mystery that he had to solve. He put his spectacles back on and tucked the handkerchief back into his pocket. He took another deep breath and then let himself out of the toilet.

"So what is happening?" asked Captain Kumar. "Can we let the passengers off?"

"I am afraid not," said Inspector Zhang. "I have been authorised to carry out an investigation. Until then, the doors remain closed."

"What assistance can I offer you?" asked the pilot.

"I will first examine the body. Then I need to speak to the Chief Purser and to whoever discovered the body." He nodded at Sergeant Lee, who was already taking out her notepad and pen. "Come with me, Sergeant," he said.

He stood in the middle of the cabin and held up his warrant card. "Ladies and gentlemen, my name is Inspector Zhang of the Singapore Police Force," he said. "As you are no doubt aware, there has been an incident on board this flight. I would be grateful if you would all stay in your seats until I have had a chance to examine the scene."

"You can't keep us here against our will!" shouted a Chinese man in a suit sitting at the rear of the cabin. There were thirty seats in the Raffles cabin, but only eight were occupied. The man who had spoken was sitting on the opposite side to where the body was, in a seat next to the window.

"I'm afraid I can," said the Inspector. "You are... ?"

"Lung Chin-po," said the man. "I have an important meeting to go to." He looked at his watch. "Immigration in Bangkok can take up to an hour, and then there's always heavy traffic. Really, I have to get off this plane now."

"I'm sorry for the inconvenience, but the doors will not be opened until the investigation has been concluded."

A heavy-set man in a tweed jacket, sitting in the middle of the cabin next to an equally large woman in a pale green trouser suit, raised a hand. "I agree with that gentleman," he said in a slow American drawl. "My wife and I are tourists, and we've got a limo waiting for us outside. What's happened obviously can't have anything to do with us. We don't know anyone in this part of the world."

Inspector Zhang pushed his spectacles up his nose. "Again, I understand how you feel, but the sooner I get on with my investigation, the sooner we can open the doors and get on our way."

The American groaned and folded his arms as he glared at the Inspector.

"Sergeant Lee, would you get the names, addresses and passport details of all the passengers, and find a floor plan with seat numbers?"

Inspector Zhang walked to the front of the cabin and headed along the bulkhead towards the blanket-covered body. A short man in a black leather jacket and impenetrable sunglasses moved his legs to allow the inspector to squeeze by. Inspector Zhang thanked him and the man nodded.

The pilot followed Inspector Zhang over to the body. It was in seat 11K. Inspector Zhang slowly pulled the pale-blue blanket away. The victim was a Thai man in his thirties, wearing a dark suit with a white shirt and a black tie. The front of the shirt was stained with blood that had pooled and congealed in the man's lap.

"This was how he was found?" asked the Inspector. "With the blood?"

"Nothing has been touched," said the Captain.

"And who discovered that he was dead?"

"It was one of the stewardesses."

"Could you get her for me, please?" said Inspector Zhang. He leant down over the body, taking a pen and using it to slide the jacket open. There was a small hole in the shirt just below the breastbone, and the shirt was peppered with tiny flecks of black. He leant closer and sniffed. Gunshot residue. The man had been shot.

As the Inspector straightened up, the pilot returned with a young stewardess. "This is Sumin," said the pilot. "She was the one who discovered that the passenger was dead."

Inspector Zhang smiled at the stewardess. "What time did you realise that there was something wrong?" he asked.

"I was checking that passengers had their seatbelts fastened, so it would have been just as we were starting our approach. That would have been about fifteen minutes before we landed."

"And what made you realise that something was wrong?"

"I thought he was asleep," said the stewardess. "I leaned over to fasten the belt and I moved his jacket. That's when I saw the blood." She shuddered. "There was so much blood."

"What did you do then?" asked the Inspector.

"I went to get the Chief Purser and he checked for a pulse, and when he didn't find one, we covered him with a blanket."

"Did you inform the pilot right away?"

"No, Mr. Yip said we should wait until we had landed."

"And did you hear anything at all unusual during the flight?"

The stewardess frowned. "Unusual?"

"A gunshot? A loud bang?"

The stewardess laughed nervously and put a hand up over her mouth. "Of course not," she said. She looked at Captain Kumar. "A gunshot?"

"There was no gunshot," said Captain Kumar. "I was sitting in the cockpit with the first officer just ten feet away. We would have heard a shot if there had been one, as would the rest of the passengers. There was no shot."

"Well, I can assure you that there is a bullet hole in the body and gunshot residue on the shirt," said Inspector Zhang. "He was shot and at close range."

"But that's impossible!" said the pilot.

"Yes," agreed Inspector Zhang. "It is. Quite impossible." He reached into the dead man's inside pocket and took out a Thai passport. He opened it and compared the picture to the face of the victim. They matched. "Kwanchai Srisai," read Inspector Zhang. "Born in Udon Thani. Thirty-seven years old." He closed the passport, handed it to Sergeant Lee and turned to look at the cabin. "The cabin appears to be almost empty," he said to the pilot. "Have some passengers moved to the rear of the plane?"

The pilot shook his head. "At this time of the year the Raffles section is rarely full," he said. "The business-class fare is quite expensive, and the flight from Singapore to Bangkok is short, so most of our passengers choose to fly economy."

Inspector Zhang did a quick head count. "Eight passengers in all, including the victim."

The pilot looked across at the stewardess. "Is that what the manifest says?"

"That is correct," she said. "Eight passengers."

"And during the flight, did any passengers from the economy section come forward to this part of the plane?"

"I don't think so," she said.

"I need to know for certain," said Inspector Zhang.

The stewardess nodded. "You will need to ask the other members of the cabin crew," she said. "I was busy in the galley for some of the flight. Twice I had to clean the toilets, and I had to go to the cockpit with coffee for Captain Kumar and the first officer."

"She did," said the Captain. "I always have a cup of coffee midway through a flight."

"Then I will need to talk to the rest of the cabin crew at some point," said Inspector Zhang. "So tell me, Miss Sumin, was everything okay with Mr. Srisai during the flight?"

"In what way, Inspector?"

"Did anything out of the ordinary happen? Before you discovered that he was dead, obviously."

"I don't think so."

"He ate his meal?"

She nodded. "Yes, and he drank a lot of champagne. He was always asking for champagne."

"And he went to the bathroom?"

"Just once. About halfway through the flight, just after I had cleared away his meal things."

"But nothing unusual?"

"No, Inspector. Nothing."

Inspector Zhang turned to Sergeant Lee. "So, Sergeant, run through the passengers for me, please."

"As you said, there are seven passengers in addition to the victim," said Sergeant Lee. She turned and pointed to a young Thai girl who was listening to music through headphones, bobbing her head back and forth in time to the music. "The lady in 14A is a Thai student, Tasanee Boontaisong. She studies in Singapore and is returning to see her parents."

Inspector Zhang frowned as he looked at the girl. "I see that there are no rows numbered 1 to 10 and that the front row of the cabin is row 11," he said. "She is in the third row; that would make it row 13, would it not?"

"There is no row 13," said Captain Kumar. "In some cultures the number 13 is considered unlucky."

Sergeant Lee looked up from her notebook. "Clearly on this flight it was number 11 that was unlucky," she said.

Inspector Zhang looked at her sternly, but she didn't appear to have been joking, merely stating a fact.

"Two rows behind Miss Boontaisong in 16A is Lung Chin-po, the Singaporean businessman you spoke to," she continued. "He says he is a friend of the Deputy Commissioner and that he will sue our department if we continue to hold him against his will."

Inspector Zhang chuckled softly. "Well, I wish him every success with that," he said.

"Those are the only two passengers sitting on the right-hand side," said Sergeant Lee: "Mr. Lung and Miss Boontaisong."

"Port," said Captain Kumar. "That's the port side. Right and left depend on which way you are facing, so on planes and boats we say port and starboard. As you face the front, port is on the left and starboard is on the right." He smiled. "It prevents confusion."

"And I am all in favour of preventing confusion," said Inspector Zhang. "So, Sergeant Lee, who is sitting in the middle of the cabin?"

The Sergeant nodded at the man in sunglasses sitting in 11F. He was sitting with his arms folded, staring straight ahead at the bulkhead. "The man there is Mr. Lev Gottesman, from Israel. He is Mr.

Srisai's bodyguard. Was, I mean. He was Mr. Srisai's bodyguard."

"And why would Mr. Srisai require the services of a bodyguard?" asked Inspector Zhang.

"I didn't ask," said Sergeant Lee. "I'm sorry. Should I have?"

"I shall question Mr. Gottesman shortly," said the Inspector. "Please continue."

Sergeant Lee pursed her lips and looked at her notebook. "In the row behind Mr. Gottesman, in seat 14A, is Andrew Yates, a British stockbroker who works for a Thai firm. He was attending a meeting in Singapore." Inspector Zhang looked over at a man in his early forties wearing a grey suit. His hair was dyed blond, and gel glistened under the cabin lights as he bent down over a BlackBerry, texting with both thumbs.

"Directly behind Mr. Yates are Mr. and Mrs. Woodhouse from Seattle in the United States. They are touring Southeast Asia. They were in Singapore for three days; they have a week in Thailand, and then they are due to fly to Vietnam and then on to China."

She nodded at the final passenger, a Thai man sitting at the back of the cabin in seat 16H, adjacent to the aisle. "Mr. Nakprakone is a journalist who works for *Thai Rath* newspaper in Bangkok. He is a Thai."

"I have heard of the paper," said Inspector Zhang. "It is one of those sensationalist papers that publish pictures of accidents and murders on their front pages, I believe."

"Mr. Nakprakone said that it sells more than a million copies every day."

"Sensationalism sells; that is true," said Inspector Zhang with a sigh. "I am personally happier with more dignified newspapers such as our own *Straits Times*. Did you ask Mr. Nakprakone why he was flying in the business-class section?"

"I didn't. Should I have done?"

"It's not a problem," said Inspector Zhang. "So, I assume you asked everyone if they heard or saw anything suspicious during the flight."

"No one did, sir."

"And I assume that no one mentioned hearing a gunshot?"

"Definitely not. Besides, sir, it would be impossible for anyone to get a gun onto a plane. There are stringent security checks at Changi."

The stewardess who had been talking to the pilot appeared at Inspector Zhang's shoulder. "Inspector Zhang, would it be all right to serve drinks and snacks to the passengers?" she asked.

"Of course," he said.

The stewardess smiled and walked to the galley.

"So, first things first," said Inspector Zhang. "We need to know why our victim was murdered. More often than not, if you know why a murder took place, you will know who committed it."

"So you want to talk to the bodyguard?"

Inspector Zhang shook his head. "I believe I will get more information from Mr. Nakprakone," he said.

Sergeant Lee scratched her head as Inspector Zhang walked to the rear of the cabin and then cut across seats D and F to get to the Thai man sitting in seat 16H. "Mr. Nakprakone?" he said. The man nodded. Inspector Zhang gestured at the empty seat by the window. "Would you mind if I sat there while I ask you a few questions?"

"Go ahead," said Mr. Nakprakone and moved his feet to allow the Inspector to squeeze by.

Inspector Zhang sat down, adjusting the creases of his trousers. "I assume you know that it is Mr. Srisai who has been murdered?"

Mr. Nakprakone nodded.

"I was wondering if you could tell me a little about Mr. Srisai."

Mr. Nakprakone frowned. "Why would you think that I would know anything about him?"

"Because you're a journalist, and because newspapers don't usually fly their staff around in business class." He smiled and shrugged. "I am in the same position. My boss told me that I had to fly economy. The Singapore Police Force is always trying to reduce costs, and I am sure that your newspaper is the same."

Mr. Nakprakone grinned. "That is exactly right," he said, speaking slowly, as if he were not entirely comfortable communicating in English.

"So am I right in assuming that you are here in the business-class section so that you could talk to him, perhaps even to interview him?"

Mr. Nakprakone nodded. He took a small digital camera from his pocket. "And to also get a photograph."

"Did you talk to him?"

"Only for a very short time. I waited for his bodyguard to go to the toilet, and then I asked Khun Srisai for an interview. He refused."

"And did you by any chance get a photograph?"

Mr. Nakprakone switched on the camera and held it out to Inspector Zhang. "Just one," he said.

Inspector Zhang looked at the screen on the back of the camera. Mr. Srisai was in his seat, holding up his hand, an angry look on his face. Inspector Zhang looked at the time code on the bottom of the picture. It had been taken thirty minutes before the plane had landed. "He obviously didn't want to be photographed," he said, handing back the camera.

"Just after I took it, the bodyguard came back, so I returned to my seat." He put the camera away.

"So tell me, why was Mr. Srisai of such interest to your paper?"

"He is a well-known gangster, but he has political aspirations," said the journalist. "There was an attempt on his life in Udon Thani two months ago, and he fled to Singapore. But last week his uncle died, and he was returning for the funeral."

"Political aspirations?"

"He had been setting up a vote-buying campaign in his home province, which could well have seen him becoming an MP in the next election. But someone put a bomb under his car and killed his driver. And shots were fired at his house at night, killing a maid."

"So he was forced to flee Thailand?"

"We think he was just hiding out while he took care of his enemies."

"Took care?"

Mr. Nakprakone made a gun from his hand and pretended to fire it. "There have been half a dozen killings in his province since he left."

Inspector Zhang nodded thoughtfully. "You think he was taking revenge?"

"I am sure of it. And so was my paper."

"So it is fair to say that a lot of people would want Mr. Srisai dead?"

Mr. Nakprakone nodded.

"You say that his uncle died. What happened?" Two stewardesses began moving down the aisles, handing out drinks and snacks.

"He was driving his motorcycle at night and he crashed. He'd been drinking, and the other driver fled the scene." He shrugged. "A common enough event in Thailand." He leaned closer to the Inspector. "So he was shot, is that right?"

"It appears so, yes."

"But that is impossible. He was perfectly all right when I spoke to him, and there have been no shots. We would have heard or seen something, wouldn't we?"

Inspector Zhang looked forward. All he could see was the back of the seat in front of him. He couldn't see Sergeant Lee or the pilot, even though he knew that they were standing at the front of the cabin. "You wouldn't have seen anything sitting here," said Inspector Zhang. "But you would of course have heard a shot, had there been one." He stood up and eased himself into the aisle. "Thank you for your help," he said.

"When can we get off the plane?" asked Mr. Nakprakone.

"As soon as I have ascertained what happened," said the Inspector. He crossed over to the far side of the cabin and walked up the aisle to where Sergeant Lee was standing with the pilot.

"I shall be writing to the Police Commissioner in Singapore," said the American tourist as Inspector Zhang walked by.

"I am acting on the Commissioner's personal instructions," said Inspector Zhang.

"Then you will be hearing from my lawyer," snapped the American.

"I shall look forward to it," said Inspector Zhang. "But in the meantime I have an investigation that requires my undivided attention." He walked away, leaving the American fuming.

Captain Kumar and Sergeant Lee were waiting expectantly by the exit door.

"The victim was a Thai gangster," Inspector Zhang said quietly. "He had a lot of enemies."

"That explains the bodyguard," whispered Sergeant Lee. The bodyguard was sitting only a few feet away, reading an in-flight magazine.

"According to the journalist, he spoke to Mr. Srisai about half an hour before the plane landed. So he must have been killed in the time between talking to the journalist and the stewardess checking that his seat belt was fastened."

"That couldn't have been much more than fifteen minutes," said Captain Kumar, rubbing his chin. He put a hand on Inspector Zhang's shoulder. "I think I should assist my first officer with the paperwork, if that is okay with you."

"Of course, Captain."

"And nobody heard anything?" Inspector Zhang asked Sergeant Lee as Captain Kumar went into the cockpit and closed the door behind him.

"Nothing," she said.

Inspector Zhang frowned. "So how can this be, Sergeant Lee? How can a man die of a gunshot wound in an aeroplane cabin without anyone hearing anything?"

"A silencer, sir?"

Inspector Zhang nodded thoughtfully. "Actually the technical term is 'suppressor,' rather than 'silencer.' And while they do deaden the sound of a gun, it would certainly still be loud enough to hear in a confined space such as this."

"Not if everyone was listening through headphones," said the Sergeant.

"A good point, Sergeant." He turned to nod at the passenger in 17D. "But Mr. Yates did not use his headphones—they are still in their sealed plastic bag—so I assume that he was working throughout the flight. Other than the bodyguard, he would have been the closest passenger to the victim. And even if a silencer was used, we have to ask ourselves how it and the gun were smuggled on board. As you said, there are stringent security screenings at the airport."

"Maybe it was a member of the crew," said the Sergeant. She lowered her voice to a whisper. "What about the Captain, sir? He could have a gun in the cockpit. Or the first officer? Or a member of the cabin crew? Mr. Yip, perhaps."

"I had considered the cabin crew, but again it comes down to the fact that the bodyguard did not see Mr. Srisai being attacked."

"Perhaps the bodyguard was not as alert as he claims. He could have been asleep." Sergeant Lee's eyes widened. "The gun," she said. "The gun must still be on the plane."

"One would assume so," said Inspector Zhang.

"We could ask the Thai police to help us find it. They must have dogs that can sniff out guns and explosives at the airport, don't you think?"

"I'm sure they have, but my instructions are to bring the investigation to a conclusion without the involvement of the Royal Thai police."

Sergeant Lee looked crestfallen, and Inspector Zhang felt a twinge of guilt at having to dampen her enthusiasm.

"But your idea is a good one, Sergeant Lee," he said. "If there were a gun on the plane, such a dog would be able to find it. But do you know what, Sergeant? I do not believe that the gun is on the plane."

Sergeant Lee frowned as she brushed a lock of hair behind her ear. "So do you now wish to interview the bodyguard?"

"I think I will first talk to Mr. Yates," said Inspector Zhang. He walked down the aisle and stood next to the Westerner, who looked up quizzically from his BlackBerry. "Mr. Yates?"

Mr. Yates nodded. "What can I do for you?"

Inspector Zhang pointed at the empty seat. "Do you mind if I sit down and ask you a few questions?"

"Of course, no problem," said Mr. Yates, making room for the Inspector to squeeze by. He put away his BlackBerry. "Do you have any idea how long this is going to take, Inspector?" he asked. "I have a meeting to get to."

"I hope not too much longer," said Inspector Zhang as he sat down. "So you are British?"

"Yes, but I haven't been to England for more than fifteen years," said Mr. Yates. "I lived in Hong Kong for a while, but I've been based in Bangkok for almost ten years."

"I am a big fan of English writers. Sir Arthur Conan Doyle, Agatha Christie, Dorothy L. Sayers, Edgar Wallace."

"I'm not a big reader," said Mr. Yates. "Never have been."

Inspector Zhang's face fell, but he managed to cover his discomfort by removing his spectacles and polishing them with his handkerchief. "So, my sergeant asked you if you saw or heard anything unusual during the flight?"

"I was working," said Mr. Yates.

"So you didn't hear a shot, for instance?"

"A shot? A gunshot? Of course not." He frowned. "Is that what happened, the guy over there was shot?"

"It appears so, yes."

"That's impossible."

"Yes, I agree. During the flight did you see anyone go over to Mr. Srisai?"

"Who?"

"I'm sorry," said Inspector Zhang. "That is the deceased's name. He is a Thai gentleman. Did you see anyone talking to him during the flight?"

"To be honest, I was busy," said Mr. Yates. "I hardly looked up. But there was a Thai man talking to him not long before we landed. They were arguing, I think." He twisted around in his seat and pointed at Mr. Nakprakone. "That guy back there."

"Arguing?"

"There was a flash, I think the man might have taken a photograph, but really I wasn't paying attention." He smiled. "I'm putting together a proposal for a client, and it has to be done by close of business today."

"You are a stockbroker?" He put his spectacles back on.

"That's right."

"Have you heard of Mr. Srisai? I gather he is active politically in Thailand."

Mr. Yates shook his head. "I'm more concerned about profit and loss accounts and dividend payments than I am with politics," he said. "The Thai political situation is so messed up that I don't think anyone really understands what's going on. It would make our lives much easier if Thailand were run more like Singapore."

Inspector Zhang nodded in agreement. "I sometimes think that the whole world would be better off if it were run like Singapore," he said.

"So he was a VIP, was he?"

"Apparently."

"That explains the run-in with security he had at Changi, then. Thai VIPs expect kid glove treatment wherever they go."

"What happened?" asked Inspector Zhang.

"I don't know, really. He was behind me at the security check, and the arch thing beeped when he went through. They wanted to search him, but he was arguing."

"Arguing about what?"

"I've no idea. I just collected my briefcase and walked away. But he was shouting about something or other."

Inspector Zhang thanked him and then stood up and rejoined Sergeant Lee at the front of the cabin.

"Is everything okay, sir?" she asked.

"Everything is satisfactory," said the Inspector.

The door to the cockpit opened and Captain Kumar came out with Mr. Yip. The pilot smiled apologetically. "I know that you said that we wouldn't be allowing anyone off the plane until your investigation has been completed, but Mr. Yip tells me that the economy-class passengers are starting to get restless," he said. "We've turned the engines off and we haven't connected to an ancillary power source yet, which means that our air-conditioning isn't on. Here in Raffles class it isn't a problem, but economy is almost full, and it's getting hot back there."

Inspector Zhang nodded thoughtfully. "I think we have almost concluded our investigation," he said.

"We have?" said Sergeant Lee, surprised.

Inspector Zhang smiled at the Chief Purser. "Mr. Yip, members of your cabin crew would have been in the galley throughout the flight, yes?"

Mr. Yip nodded. "Of course."

"Then I need you to confirm with them that at no point did any of the economy passengers move through the galley to the front cabin."

"They wouldn't have been allowed to," said Mr. Yip. "Not even to use the toilet. We insist that economy-class passengers remain in the economy cabin."

"I understand, but I would like you to confirm that for me," said the Inspector.

Mr. Yip nodded and hurried back to the galley.

"Captain Kumar, would it be possible for the passengers to disembark from the rear of the plane?"

"It wouldn't be a problem, though we would have to bring out a stairway," said the pilot.

"If the economy passengers are getting off, then we should be allowed to get off with them," said Mr. Woodhouse from his seat in the middle of the cabin.

"I'm afraid that's not possible," said Inspector Zhang.

Mr. Woodhouse waved a blue passport in the air. "I'm an American citizen," he said. "You can't keep us prisoners like this."

"That's right," agreed his wife.

"We're just tourists. This is nothing to do with us," said Mr. Woodhouse.

"Exactly!' said his wife.

"I am sorry for the inconvenience," said Inspector Zhang.

"Being sorry doesn't cut it," said the American. "This isn't fair. You're saying that if we had flown economy you'd let us off, but because we bought business-class tickets you're keeping us prisoner." He jabbed a thick finger at the Inspector. "I demand that the American ambassador be informed of this immediately."

"Immediately!" echoed Mrs. Woodhouse.

"Please, Mr. Woodhouse, Mrs. Woodhouse, just bear with us," said Inspector Zhang calmly. "This will all be resolved shortly."

Mr. Yip came back down the aisle. "I have spoken to all the cabin crew, and I have their assurance that no passengers left the economy cabin throughout the flight."

"In that case, Captain, I have no objection to your allowing the economy passengers to disembark from the rear of the plane."

"I'm going too," said the Chinese businessman. He stood up and opened the locker above his head to pull out a Louis Vuitton briefcase.

"I am afraid I must ask you to remain in your seat for a little while longer, Mr. Lung," said Inspector Zhang.

Mr. Lung turned to look at the Inspector, his upper lip curled back in a snarl. "No," he said. "I've been here long enough. This is Thailand. You've no jurisdiction here. You do not have the authority to keep me on this plane."

"You might well be right, Mr. Lung," said the Inspector. "But of one thing I am sure: immediately you step out of this plane, the Thai police will have the authority to arrest you, and I will make sure that they do just that. And I am also sure that you would not appreciate the inside of a Thai prison, because that is where you will be held until this investigation is complete."

"This is an outrage," snapped the businessman, but he went back to his seat.

"I agree," said Inspector Zhang. "Murder is an outrage. Which is why I want to solve this murder as quickly as possible. Once the perpetrator has been apprehended, we can all leave the plane."

The bodyguard was sitting in his seat, staring at the bulkhead. He didn't look up as Inspector Zhang sat down next to him in seat 11D. "You are Mr. Lev Gottesman," he said.

The man nodded but said nothing.

"From Israel?"

"From Tel Aviv."

"And you were employed by Mr. Srisai, as a bodyguard?"

The man turned his head slowly until Inspector Zhang could see his own reflection in the impenetrable lenses of the man's sunglasses. "Is that some sort of a wisecrack?" he said, his voice a hoarse whisper.

"I am merely trying to ascertain the facts in this case," said Inspector Zhang.

The man's lips formed a tight line and then he nodded slowly. "Yes, I was hired to be his bodyguard. And yes, the fact that he's dead means I did not do a good job." He folded his arms and stared at the bulkhead again.

"Mr. Gottesman, I would like you to remove your sunglasses, please."

"Why?"

"Because I like to see a man's eyes when he is talking to me. The eyes, after all, are the windows to the soul."

The Israeli took off his glasses, folded them and put them into the inside pocket of his leather jacket.

"Thank you," said Inspector Zhang. "And if you would be so good as to give me your passport." The bodyguard reached into his pocket and handed the Inspector a blue passport. "How long have you been in Mr. Srisai's employ?"

"About eight weeks."

"And your predecessor was killed?"

The Israeli nodded. "There was a car bomb. The bodyguard was driving. Bodyguards should never drive. Drivers drive and bodyguards take care of security. Mr. Srisai did not take his own safety seriously enough."

"Your predecessor was Thai?"

The Israeli nodded again. "They are not well trained, the Thais. They think that any soldier or cop can be a bodyguard, but the skills are different."

"And your skills, where do they come from? You were a soldier?"

The bodyguard sneered. "All Israelis are soldiers. Our country is surrounded by enemies."

"More than a soldier, then? Mossad? Did you use to work for the Israeli intelligence service?"

The Israeli nodded but said nothing. Inspector Zhang flicked through the passport.

"So you are a professional," said Inspector Zhang. "As a professional, what do you think happened?"

"He died. I failed. And as for being a professional, I doubt that anyone will employ me again after this."

Sergeant Lee appeared at Inspector Zhang's side, taking notes. "And you saw nothing?" asked the Inspector.

The bodyguard turned to stare at Inspector Zhang with eyes that were a blue so pale they were almost grey. "If I had seen anything, do you think I would have allowed it to happen?" he said.

"Obviously not. And equally, you heard nothing?"

"Of course I heard nothing."

"So what do you think happened, Mr. Gottesman? Who killed your client?"

"He had many enemies."

"So I gather. But are any of those enemies on this plane?"

"He didn't see any while we were waiting to board."

"But you would have been in the VIP lounge, would you not? So you wouldn't have seen everyone."

"True," said the Israeli. "But the only people in the forward cabin are those with business-class tickets. It couldn't have been anyone from the rear of the plane, could it?"

"I agree," said Inspector Zhang. "Now when was the last time you saw him alive?"

"I went to the toilet shortly before landing. I came back to find that journalist pestering Mr. Srisai. Then I read a magazine. Then the stewardess came around to tell us to fasten our seat belts, and when she checked Mr. Srisai, she realised something was wrong. She fetched the guy in the suit, and he said he was dead and covered him with a blanket."

"You didn't check for yourself?"

"They told me to stay in my seat. They said there was nothing I could do."

Inspector Zhang nodded thoughtfully. "Was he an easy man to work for?"

The bodyguard shrugged. "He liked to do things his own way."

"So he was difficult?"

"I wouldn't say difficult."

"There was an argument at security back at the airport, I'm told."

"It was nothing. A misunderstanding."

"About what?"

"The metal detector beeped. They searched him. I think it was his watch that set it off. He wears a big gold Rolex."

"And there was an argument?"

"He didn't want to be stopped. Men like Mr. Srisai, they are used to getting their own way."

"And while you were in Singapore, where did you stay?"

"We moved from hotel to hotel, changing every few days. Last night we stayed at the Sheraton."

"Because Mr. Srisai was concerned for his safety?"

The bodyguard nodded. "He said there were people who still wanted him dead, even though he had left Thailand."

"But nothing happened during the flight to give you any cause for concern?"

"That's right. I was stunned when they said he was dead. I don't know how it could have happened."

Inspector Zhang handed the bodyguard his passport. "You say that you have only worked for Mr. Srisai for two months."

"That's correct."

"But I see from the visas in your passport that you only arrived from Israel two months ago."

The bodyguard put away the passport. "That's right. I was hired over the phone and flew out to take up the position."

"But you had never met before then?"

The bodyguard shook his head. "A friend of Mr. Srisai recommended me. We spoke on the phone and agreed on terms, and I flew straight out to Thailand. Shortly after I arrived, shots were fired at his house and a maid was killed, so he decided to fly to Singapore."

Inspector Zhang smiled. "Well, thank you for your time," he said. He stood up and patted Sergeant Lee on the arm. "Come with me," he said and took her through the galley and into the economy cabin, which was almost empty. The cabin crew were shepherding the few remaining passengers out of the door at the rear of the plane. "I think it best we speak here, so that the passengers cannot hear us," he said. "So what do you think, Sergeant?"

She shrugged and opened her notebook. "I don't know, sir, I just don't know. We have an impossible situation, a crime that could not have happened and yet clearly has happened."

"Very succinctly put, Sergeant," said Inspector Zhang.

"We know that the victim couldn't have been shot on the plane. That would have been impossible."

"That is true," said Inspector Zhang.

"But if he had been shot before he boarded, why was there no blood? And how could a man with a bullet in his chest get onto the plane, eat his meal and go to the toilet? That would be impossible, too."

"Again, that is true," agreed the Inspector.

"So it's impossible," said Sergeant Lee, flicking through her notebook. "The only solutions are impossible ones."

Inspector Zhang held up his hand. "Then at this point we must consider the words of Sherlock Holmes in "The Adventure of the Beryl Coronet," by Sir Arthur Conan Doyle. For in that book the great detective lays down one of the great truths of detection—once you eliminate the impossible, whatever remains, no matter how improbable, must be the truth."

Sergeant Lee frowned. "But how does that help us if everything is impossible?"

"No, Sergeant. Everything cannot be impossible because we have a victim and we have a crime scene, and we also have a murderer that we have yet to identify. What we have to do is to eliminate the impossible, and that we have done. We know that he was killed on the plane. That is certain because he was alive for most of the flight. So it was impossible for him to have been killed before boarding. But we are equally certain that it was impossible for him to have been shot while he was sitting in the cabin."

"Exactly," said Sergeant Lee. "It's impossible. The whole thing is impossible." She snapped her notebook shut in frustration.

Inspector Zhang smiled. "Not necessarily," he said quietly. "We have eliminated the impossible, so we are left with the truth. If he was not shot on the plane, then he must have been shot before he boarded. That is the only possibility."

"Okay," said the Sergeant hesitantly.

"And if he did not die before boarding, then he must have been murdered on the plane."

The Sergeant shrugged.

"So the only possible explanation is that he was shot before he boarded and was murdered on the plane." Inspector Zhang pushed his spectacles up his nose. "I know that those two statements appear to be mutually exclusive, but it is the only possible explanation." He took out his cell phone. "I must use my phone," he said and headed towards the rear of the plane.

The pilot came up to Sergeant Lee, and they both watched as Inspector Zhang talked into his cell phone, his hand cupped around his mouth.

"Is he always like this?" asked Captain Kumar.

"Like what?" asked Sergeant Lee.

"Secretive," said the pilot. "As if he doesn't want anyone else to know what's going on."

"I think Inspector Zhang does not like to be wrong," she said. "So until he is sure, he holds his own counsel."

"Do you think he knows who the killer is?"

"If anyone does, it is Inspector Zhang," she said.

They waited until Inspector Zhang had finished, but when he did put the phone away, he turned his back on them and headed out of the door at the back of the plane.

"Now where is he going?" asked Captain Kumar.

"I have absolutely no idea," said Sergeant Lee.

After a few minutes the Inspector returned, followed by two brown-uniformed Thai policemen with large handguns in holsters and gleaming black boots.

"Is everything all right, Inspector?" asked the pilot.

"Everything is perfect," said Inspector Zhang. "I am now in a position to hand the perpetrator of the crime over to the Thai authorities." He strode past them and headed towards the front of the plane. Captain Kumar and Sergeant Lee fell into step behind the two Thai police officers.

Inspector Zhang stopped at the front of the cabin and looked down at the bodyguard, who was sipping a glass of orange juice. "So, Mr. Gottesman, I now understand everything," he said.

The Israeli shrugged.

"The confrontation at the security checkpoint at Changi Airport was nothing to do with your client's watch, was it?"

"It was his watch. It set off the alarm," said the bodyguard.

"No, Mr. Gottesman, it was not his watch. And you should know that I have only just finished talking to the head of security at the airport."

The bodyguard slowly put down his glass of orange juice.

"Your client was wearing a bullet-proof vest under his shirt, and he was told by security staff that he could not wear it on the plane. Isn't that the case, Mr. Gottesman?"

The Israeli said nothing and his face remained a blank mask.

"They made him remove the bullet-proof jacket and check it into the hold," said Inspector Zhang.

"If that happened, I didn't see it. I'd already left the security area."

"Nonsense. You are a professional bodyguard. Your job requires you to stay with him at all times. No bodyguard would leave his client's side. And I also spoke to the hotel where Mr. Srisai stayed. There were reports of a shot this morning. A gunshot. At the hotel."

The bodyguard shrugged carelessly. "That's news to me," he said.

Inspector Zhang and the Dead Thai Gangster

Inspector Zhang's eyes hardened. "It is time to stop lying, Mr. Gottesman."

"I'm not lying. Why would I lie?"

Inspector Zhang pointed a finger at the bodyguard's face. "I know everything, Mr. Gottesman, so lying is futile. You were with Mr. Srisai when he was shot. The chief of security at the hotel told me as much."

"So?"

"So I need you to explain the circumstances of the shooting to me."

The bodyguard sighed and folded his arms. "We left the hotel. We were heading to the car. Out of nowhere this guy appeared with a gun. He shot Mr. Srisai in the chest and ran off."

"Which is when you realised that your client was wearing a bullet-proof vest under his shirt."

The bodyguard nodded.

"And that came as a surprise to you, did it not?"

"He hadn't told me he was wearing a vest, if that's what you mean."

"The vest that saved his life."

The bodyguard nodded but didn't say anything.

"Can you explain to me why the police were not called?"

"Mr. Srisai said not to. The shooter ran off. Then we heard a motorbike. He got clean away. He'd been wearing a mask, so we didn't know what he looked like. Mr. Srisai said he just wanted to get out of Singapore."

"And he wasn't hurt?"

"Not a scratch. He fell back when he was shot, but he wasn't hurt."

"And you went straight to the airport?"

"He didn't want to miss his flight."

"And he didn't wait to change his clothes?"

"That's right. He said we were to get into the car and go. He was worried that the police would be involved and they wouldn't allow him to leave the country."

Inspector Zhang turned to look at Sergeant Lee. "Which explains why there was a bullet hole in the shirt and gunpowder residue."

Sergeant Lee nodded and scribbled in her notebook. Then she stopped writing and frowned. "But if he was wearing a bullet-proof vest, how did he die?" she asked.

Inspector Zhang looked at the bodyguard. Beads of sweat had formed on the Israeli's forehead, and he was licking his lips nervously. "My Sergeant raises a good point, doesn't she, Mr. Gottes-man?"

"This is nothing to do with me," said the bodyguard.

"Oh, it is everything to do with you," said Inspector Zhang. "You are a professional, trained by the Mossad. You are the best of the best, are you not?"

"That's what they say," said the Israeli.

"So perhaps you can explain how an assassin got so close to your client that he was able to shoot him in the chest?"

"He took us by surprise," said the bodyguard.

"And how did the assassin know where your client was?"

The bodyguard didn't reply.

"You were moving from hotel to hotel. And I am assuming that Mr. Srisai did not broadcast the fact that he was flying back to Bangkok today."

The bodyguard's lips had tightened into a thin, impenetrable line.

"Someone must have told the assassin where and when to strike. And that someone can only be you."

"You can't prove that," said the bodyguard quietly.

Inspector Zhang nodded slowly. "You are probably right," he said.

"So why are we wasting our time here?"

"Because it is what happened on board this plane that concerns me, Mr. Gottesman. Mr. Srisai was not injured in the attack outside the hotel. But he is now dead. And you killed him."

The bodyguard shook his head. "You can't possibly prove that. And anyway, why would I want to kill my client?"

Inspector Zhang shrugged. "I am fairly sure that I can prove it," he said. "And so far as motive goes,

I think it is probably one of the oldest motives in the world. Money. I think you were paid to kill Mr. Srisai."

"Ridiculous!" snapped the bodyguard.

"I think that when Mr. Srisai's former bodyguard was killed, someone close to Mr. Srisai used the opportunity to introduce you. That person was an enemy that Mr. Srisai thought was a friend. And that someone paid you, not to guard Mr. Srisai, but to arrange his assassination. But your first plan failed because, unbeknown to you, Mr. Srisai was wearing a bullet-proof vest."

"All this is hypothetical," said the bodyguard. "You have no proof."

"When Mr. Srisai passed through the security check, he was told to remove his vest. Which gave you an idea, didn't it? You realised that if you could somehow deal him a killing blow through the bullet hole in his shirt, then you would have everybody looking at an impossible murder. And I have no doubt that when you got off the plane, you would have been on the first flight out of the country." He turned to look at Sergeant Lee. "Israel never extradites its own citizens," he said. "Once back on Israeli soil, you would be safe."

"But why kill him on the plane?" asked Sergeant Lee. "Why not wait?"

"Because Mr. Srisai was not a stupid man. He would have come to the same conclusion that I reached—namely, that Mr. Gottesman was the only person who could have set up this morning's assassination attempt. And I am sure that he was planning retribution on his return to Thailand." He looked over the top of his spectacles at the sweating bodyguard. "I'm right, aren't I, Mr. Gottesman? You knew that as soon as you arrived in Thailand, Mr. Srisai would enact his revenge and have you killed?"

"I'm saying nothing," said the bodyguard. "You have no proof. No witnesses. You have nothing but a theory. A ridiculous theory."

"That may be so," said Inspector Zhang. "But you have the proof, don't you? On your person?"

The bodyguard's eyes narrowed and he glared at the Inspector with undisguised hatred.

"It would of course be impossible for you or anyone to bring a gun on board. And equally impossible to bring a knife. Except for a very special knife, of course. The sort of knife that someone trained by Mossad would be very familiar with." He paused, and the briefest flicker of a smile crossed his lips before he continued. "A Kevlar knife, perhaps. Or one made from carbon fibre. A knife that can pass through any security check without triggering the alarms."

"Pure guesswork," sneered the bodyguard.

Inspector Zhang shook his head. "Educated guesswork," he said. "I know for a fact that you killed Mr. Srisai because you were the last person to see him alive. You went over to him after the journalist went back to his seat, and you must have killed him then. You went to the toilet to prepare your weapon, and when you came back, you leant over Mr. Srisai and stabbed him through the hole that had been left by the bullet that had struck his vest earlier in the day. You probably put one hand over his mouth to stifle any sound he might have made. With your skills I have no doubt that you would know how to kill him instantly.

The bodyguard looked up at Captain Kumar. "Do I have to listen to this nonsense?" he asked.

"I am afraid you do," said the pilot.

"I know you have the knife on your person, Mr. Gottesman, because you have been sitting in that seat ever since Mr. Srisai was killed," said Inspector Zhang. He held out his hand. "Either you can give it to me, or these Thai police officers can take it from you. It is your choice."

The bodyguard stared at Inspector Zhang for several seconds. Then he slowly bent down and slipped his hand into his left trouser leg before pulling out a black carbon fibre stiletto knife. He held it, with the tip pointing at Inspector Zhang's chest. Then with a sigh he reversed the weapon and gave it to him.

Inspector Zhang took the knife between his thumb and finger. There was congealed blood on the blade. Sergeant Lee already had a clear plastic bag open for him, and he dropped the knife into it.

Inspector Zhang stood up, and the two Thai policemen pulled the bodyguard to his feet. He put up no resistance as they led him away.

"So the Thai police will take over the case?" asked Sergeant Lee.

"The victim was Thai. The murderer is Israeli. The crime was committed in Thai airspace. I think it best the Thais handle it."

"And the Commissioner will be satisfied with that?"

Inspector Zhang smiled. "I think so far as the plane is allowed to fly back to Singapore, the Commissioner will be happy," he said.

Sergeant Lee closed her notebook and put it away. "You solved an impossible mystery, Inspector Zhang."

"Yes, I did," agreed the Inspector. "But the real mystery is who recommended Mr. Gottesman in the first place, and I fear that is one mystery that will never be solved."

"Perhaps you could offer to help the Thai police with the investigation."

Inspector Zhang's smile widened. "What a wonderful idea, Sergeant. I shall offer them my services."

Stephen Leather

Stephen Leather is one of the UK's most successful thriller writers. Before becoming a novelist he was a journalist for more than ten years on newspapers such as *The Times*, the *Daily Mail* and the *South China Morning Post* in Hong Kong. Before that, he was employed as a biochemist for ICI, shovelled limestone in a quarry, worked as a baker, a petrol pump attendant, a barman, and worked for the Inland Revenue. He began writing full time in 1992. His bestsellers have been translated into more than ten languages. He has also written for television shows such as *London's Burning*, *The Knock* and the BBC's *Murder in Mind* series and two of his books, *The Stretch* and *The Bombmaker*, were filmed for TV.

Find out more from his website, www.stephenleather.com.

Thousand and One Nights

Pico Iyer

Dear Susan,

There were people coming at me from every side, more people than I can describe, from every corner of the world. Large Arab men in their smocks and gowns, teams of Japanese businessmen in suits, men who looked like they'd been left over from the Vietnam War and earringed couples who could have been from anywhere—all of them thronging down this lane of lights and looking into the entrances, into red-lit magic caves, all smoke and noise, to see if they could spot a Chinese princess. There's one area—you wouldn't believe it (or maybe you would; I suppose the place has become quite a legend now)—where they have whole Arabian palaces on a dark lane, furnished with great chandeliered rooms full of divans and men in gallabeahs smoking hubble-bubbles, while girls of every shape and size move among them, from one dream chamber to the next, looking for a touch of magic, a month's salary in a night's adventure.

Anyway, you know all about Bangkok already. And this isn't the kind of thing one would ordinarily be telling a sister. But since Sarah went away—well, you know how it is. Nobody will listen to me, or if they do, they listen in a way that says they're only being kind or doing their charity work for the day. You're the only one who understands. I tell myself that talking to you is like talking to a better version of myself.

So there I was in the Arabian Nights. It sounds mad, I know, but I felt as if I'd fallen into some other kind of world that was waiting beside me the way a shadow might, like those stories Nana used to read us in the nursery. Remember Alice in her rabbit hole, ending up on the underside of the world? Or the little girl who went to sleep and woke up in another place? I suppose it's what people get when they pop those pills you told me about in the disco, or shoot themselves full of the *yaa baa*, or "mad medicine," that the taxi drivers talk about here, but for someone like me—well, it all came as something of a shock.

Plus, of course, I was jet-lagged. Walking and walking through the streets after dark and looking for lunch at 3:00 a.m. Everything took on a different aspect, as if—how can I put it?—well, as if I weren't seeing the lights, really, only their reflections in a puddle. Everything blurred and shimmery and reflecting. I'd look at my face in the shop windows, and I wouldn't know who it was looking back at me. As if I'd left my self—my regular daily self—in England and now some kind of outline or facsimile was playing me, off the ground and weightless, in a trance.

The noise from the bars, the boys coming up and trying to pull me into their caves. "Here, sir, very good," "Come here, no problem, only looking." I'd turn a corner and end up in a little lane that opened up onto the river, the shining golden pinnacle of a stupa at the other end. And then I'd stumble back, and there were all these signs—Bad Boy, Helicopter, The Alternative—and you could imagine you were in the mind of a magician. Aladdin's cave, I thought.

So anyway, I walked and walked, all night, it seemed, and at one point I went into this little alley-way—lights, girls in bikinis, people selling elixirs of some kind in bottles—and I stopped off in a trattoria (they have everything here) for lunch. Outside, on the street, there were flocks of girls rather vamping it up: with long hair that swung below their shoulders, long slim legs, high heels, leopard-skin shorts, the lot.

They were cavorting up and down the street, having fun, really, occasionally stepping into a pool hall, red-lit, or one of the open-air bars that look out onto the street; once, one of them came and stood looking at me where I sat, eating on the terrace. Looking at me very directly, half-pout and half-caress.

"Where you come from, mister? What you need?"

"Nothing. I'm just passing the time, really." I sounded foolish, I knew, but I didn't know how to sound here.

"No want la-dee?" The way she said it was itself a sort of insinuation.

"No, thank you. I'm here on business."

"Same-same," she said, "business," and let out a husky laugh. "Business, pleasure, same-same. You show me good heart, I show you good time."

"I'm sure," I said. "Maybe tomorrow."

"Tomorrow," she said, as if we'd shared an illicit joke.

"You no go with ladee?" said the waiter, as the woman walked away.

"No go," I said, and then wondered why exactly I was speaking like one of them.

I looked around me, then, and realized I'd never seen so many beautiful women in one place before; then I looked closer and realized why they were so beautiful. They weren't real. They were real people, of course, just not real girls. And yet not not-real either. Some of them, I thought, just made themselves up as girls. But some were no doubt on the way to becoming real women, in every way. And some of them had completed the transformation and now, reborn, were more girlish than any girl could be. All the excitement of them came from this sense of ambiguity, of mystery, I suppose. I felt almost seasick watching them.

I went back to my hotel then—it was on one of those brightly lit lanes, which in the daytime turns out to be just a rather peeling, derelict back alleyway. But at night it is enchantment. They call this place the "City of Angels," but I think that's a kind of spell, a way of saying it's not a place of djinns. Didn't Nana tell us, one of those long winter afternoons—Scheherazade in Somerset—that the best devils in the world are the ones who look like angels?

I suppose you'll say all this has something to do with Sarah, and finding myself alone again. A widower is a king exiled from his palace, I tell my friends, and they look at one another and tell themselves I've lost it. But it's true. When you're suddenly alone again, it's as if you've lost not just your jewels, but yourself, your life. You've woken up in a strange place, and there's no way to find the road back to the castle. Nothing makes sense, and you don't have any money on you, and whatever past you thought you had is locked up in somebody else's keeping. I suppose I realized that if everyone was going to misunderstand me in any case, I might as well go full hog and become someone entirely unexpected.

Which brings me to the part that's going to shock you. I feel strange saying all this to you; I suppose if would be easier to call. But if I could hear your voice, I don't think I'd be able to say anything at all. And anyway, with you off in Bangalore, I'd probably hear someone else's voice, or someone pretending to be you. And you're not who you usually are either, I imagine, in that tropical setting, with all those streets around.

Besides, there is something rather magical about coming into one of these little cafés at 1:00 a.m.—the young girl at the desk curtsies, the kids wait around in chairs, as if waiting to be claimed—and typing these words onto a screen, and then, that very minute, the same words appear on a screen in India, taken there by a genie with STD connections.

So, back to the part where you've got to block your eyes (or ears, or both). I asked myself, as I went out for breakfast that second night, what I really wanted here. The streets around me were thronged; they have this night market thing here which is a kind of Oriental bazaar in the dark, so mad with flickering neon and shouted prices that you can hardly walk. People are shooting numbers back and forth, or offering one another calculators on which their bids are typed. Girls are drifting out of the bars in underwear, or even less. People are selling blacklight posters, lanterns, false perfumes and little vials of something strange, bras, luminous green rings to wear around your neck and spices that are said to be love potions. All around, on every corner. And I, walking through the midst of it, thought, "What is it that I could do here that I could never do at home?"

What I'm going to tell you won't make you very comfortable. But I suppose I was after something that's the opposite of comfort; if it had been comfort I wanted, I'd have stayed in London. No, I thought; this is a chance—my best chance, maybe my last chance—to become someone different. To say abracadabra and whirl myself around so fast that the person who gets up again is someone other. You know how my reasoning works when there's no real reason behind it.

People were pushing me, scraping past me as I walked, picking up panties and Rolex watches that cost less than a drink, fingering X-rated videos and bottles of Chanel that looked like colored water, and at last, having fortified myself with a beer, I went up to two girls I'd seen the night before. One of them had short, spiky hair—she was less tall than I was—and a soft, young face, virginal in a way. The other was much taller than both of us, with long hair and a tiger's face, predatory and strong.

"What magic tricks do you offer?" I said, not meaning anything, I think.

They looked at one another—though I'm sure they're used to worse—and then the small one, the shy one, said, "What country you come from?"

"England," I said.

"Same-same, America."

"Not really, no."

"Where you stay Bangkok?"

"The Dream Palace. Over near the Golden Temple."

They looked at one another appraisingly.

"You have ladee, Bangkok?"

"No," I told the shorter one. "No lady at all."

Here the taller one grabbed hold of my arm.

"You come with me," she said.

"No," said the other. "You come with me. Number one."

"Same-same," said the first. "You take us both."

"I will," I said, and the whole conversation stopped for a moment. Whatever they were expecting, it wasn't this. It wasn't what I was expecting, either. It was the moment speaking, taking me wherever it went.

They looked at me and the tall one said, "You want me and my friend?"

"Of course," I said. I don't know why, but I thought at that moment of what I'd read about the women in those poor African countries—São Tomé, the Central African Republic—who support their families by pretending to be other women at phone-sex centers. Purring down the international phone lines, as if they were in Croydon or Atlanta or somewhere, sighing and giving back false names, so they can go home and give their mothers enough money for food.

It's degrading, people will tell you. It's just colonialism in another form. It's a way of keeping the poor poor, and exploiting the fact they're in need. Maybe it is, but that wasn't how it seemed just then. The girls were eager; they didn't want to spend any longer waiting for someone who might be even worse than me. And the next thing I knew, they were leading me, one by each arm, down the little lane, past the booths and the fortune tellers and the girls in briefs, who were running a finger down a man's shirt or underneath it to his skin. It was like walking through a stranger's imagination.

We arrived a few minutes later at an unlit staircase and walked up into the dark. At the top we came to this musty aquarium of a place, with a string of lights along the walls. A man—a boy, really—was sitting at a cash register, eating something from a bowl and watching a television set that sat on the floor in a corner. With rabbit-ear antennae and a scratchy old black-and-white film on the small screen.

I suppose the girls had been here before (I call them girls because I don't know what else to call them). They collected a key from the boy, and then the three of us walked, or straggled, down the corridor. There were pink lights above every door, no windows at the end. One of them turned the old-fashioned key and we walked into this room of wonders, really; she turned on a light, and we saw a television set, a drinks cabinet, a video player, a karaoke mike. There was a deep bathtub in the middle of the room. The other girl, the smaller one, pushed another button and the room shone red, then blue.

The taller girl went into the bathroom, and the small one began to unbutton her shirt.

"No," I said, putting a hand on her arm. "Not now."

She sat on the bed—she looked puzzled, even rejected—and a few seconds later, the taller girl came out, freshly showered, with some exotic perfume newly applied. She'd changed into a bathrobe, but she hadn't done it up, so she walked across the room like someone from a James Bond film, her robe waiting to fall open.

"A thousand and one nights," I said, rather foolishly, again, and they looked at one another, a little alarmed. I suppose they were wondering—worried—what would come next.

"You crazy guy," said the tall one, pushing me onto the bed.

The other one, always more obliging, said, "No, shy. Same-same Japanese."

"No," I said. "I know what I want."

They both looked at me, expectant. All three of us were on the bed now and the red light made us feel like X-rays or something not quite real.

"We tell each other stories. The stories of our lives."

"You cheap Charlie!" said the tall one, guessing, I suppose, that this was some kind of trick. So I pulled out my red and purple notes and gave them a whole stash in advance.

They relaxed a little, and the smaller one said, "You want, we do."

"My wish is your command," I said emptily. The tall one—she was lying between us now, and her legs stretched almost to the end of the bed—said she'd always wanted to be a girl. She'd always felt incomplete somehow—a broken jug, she seemed to gesture—and when she'd been very young, she'd made a promise to herself that if she ever got the chance, she'd follow her dream right through. So she saved her money and came to the city, and made more money here, and—well, now she was what she'd always wanted to be. Her story had a happy ending.

The other one, sweeter—I liked her more—said something about a "Mama" and a child, and her promise to keep them healthy by going to the big city. She'd come here and found that men weren't very much in demand in the City of Angels. A month's wages for a construction worker's job would give her pennies to send home. And she'd thought of her mother waiting, her promise, and then she'd decided to take a gamble.

There was a knock on the door then. I suppose our allotted time was up, and I called back, "We'll pay for the whole night—tomorrow, too," and there was the sound of receding footsteps. And the girl said she'd taken her gamble. She'd passed through the mirror, and now her mother had a new house; her daughter was at school.

Then they looked at me, and I told them everything. The things I couldn't tell my friends, the things it had been hard for me to tell even you. About Sarah, I mean, and what I learned about her after she died. What I learned about myself. What I did in the house alone, what I thought of doing. All of it: everything that had been waiting to come out for nine months—263 days. I even told them how I'd said to you, that afternoon in the park, "What I really want is a genie," and you'd said, "You'd better go abroad. They don't do genies in central London."

They do, actually, now—they do everything, everywhere—but I thought that sisters know best. And then I told them about my saving my money and coming away from the city, and away from my family, towards what I knew nothing about. I suppose they were bored—it was almost light now, and we could see the colors changing through the little window, which looked out onto a wall—but they looked as if they were interested, and when I was finished, the small one leaned forward and kissed me on the cheek. The other one—Jin, she told me her name was (the smaller one was Nit)—asked me if I had a handkerchief. I gave her mine, and she brushed at her eyes a little. Something in the night had moved her.

We'd overstayed our deposit, of course, but I'm not sure that any of us wanted to go. It was cool in the room, and it was quiet; the lights made everything different. Finally the tall one said, "Go home now," and we went down to where the street was empty, just overturned tables and rubbish in the thin grey light, and a sort of bulldozer machine that noisily went back and forth, back and forth, collecting all the relics of the night. It was like coming back to something real after a night in a very different country.

The girls took me to a tuk-tuk, one of these four-wheeled rickshaws they have here, and bargained on my behalf with the boy in the front seat; they were going to go home on the backs of motorcycle taxis across the street. "You good man," said Jin. "You want meet again, you call." And, taking a flyer from a McDonald's nearby, she scribbled down her number on the back of an advert for a Happy Meal.

"I see you tonight? Same place?" said Nit, and I said, "Who knows? Maybe you will."

I got into the back of the rickshaw then and sat under the red light, as the boy banged his horn and reeled into the traffic. In daytime the magic of the city was gone, except this time it wasn't gone at all—only postponed, perhaps. The djiinn was beside me on the seat—the djinn was inside me—and this evening, or tomorrow night, or the evening after that, anything, everything seemed possible. Just telling your story, I thought: could any crime be so secret?

Photo credit: Derek Shapton

Pico Iyer

Pico Iyer is the author of several books about globalism and travel, including *Video Night in Kathmandu, The Lady and the Monk, The Global Soul* and *The Open Road*. Based in Asia since 1987, he first visited Thailand in 1983, and has since been back to Bangkok more than 50 times. Since 1992, he's been living in rural Japan.

Halfhead

Colin Cotterill

Samart Wichaiwong, a.k.a. Teacher Wong, awoke to
find his legs off the mattress and flailing. It was as if his
conscious self was fleeing his subconscious in panic. It
wasn't the first time Halfhead had chased him out of a
dream. She was no man's fantasy. She always reminded
him of the he-'n-she act at the transvestite cabarets.
The singer, tucked between the stage curtains, turns
to the left and he's a man, to the right and she's a
woman. Remarkable. Except Halfhead turns to the
left and she's a *Gray's Anatomy* centerfold. One side
of her skull is missing, sliced down the center like a
severe homicidal parting. One red eye, half a nose,
left-sided mouth with a sluggy-black tongue spilling
out. But it was the drool that really repulsed him.
The drool. Samart slapped away the memory of his
nightmare and stumbled around his apartment in
search of the remains of a bottle of Archa beer, a
refugee from last night's binge. He chugged it down.
It didn't taste any better than the scum in his mouth,
but he needed nutrition. He changed out of his striped

pajama bottom and into his white silks. His belly formed a third trimester mound inside the smock top. He swept back hair that hung like a hula skirt from his bald dome and tied it behind his neck with a rubber band. Finally, with all the artistry of a *likay* performer, he sat at the mirror and encircled his bulging eyes with a crimson bruise of lipstick. He checked the time, then took off his watch and placed it beside the DVD player. He walked untidily down to the ground floor, across the vacant lot, and unlocked the door to the humble bamboo hut in which he supposedly lived. He was early but he knew this could be a most significant day.

The two latte-brown uniformed officers were seated in front of the stage on an itchy grass mat staring at Samart, who sat cross-legged and apparently comatose on a flat cushion facing them. He was surrounded by porcelain animals, pickled reptiles gazing drowsily from glass containers, coloured vials and bottles and skulls of all sizes, animal and human. The hut's curtain was drawn, and a small fish tank lamp illuminated Samart from below, casting a campfire shadow that bent all his features upward. His red, up-all-night eyes stared dully into space. It was an image that had impressed many but obviously wasn't having a positive effect on today's audience.

"How long are we supposed to sit here like mutton?" the Colonel asked. He was in his forties, sturdy, and his looks were as ugly as his manners.

"He'll come out of it soon, sir," his captain told him. Captain Pairot was a skinny version of the Colonel but with skin as loose as lettuce. Given the common Thai propensity to subscribe heavily to police corruption, he'd no doubt fill it out soon enough.

"His soul will become aware of our presence here on earth and leave the Otherworld to join us," he said.

"Is that right? Take long, will it?"

"Could be half an hour."

"Hmm, sorry, I can't wait that long."

The Colonel unholstered his pistol, aimed and shot the head off a plaster giraffe. The bullet passed through the bamboo wall and probably wounded one of the stray dogs that loitered in the lane outside. Teacher Wong didn't appear to care, or flinch or blink. The Colonel leveled the weapon at Samart's head and started counting down from five. The shaman was out of his trance at three-and-a-half.

"Ah, officers," he said. "Have I kept you waiting long?"

"Yes," grunted the Colonel, reholstering his gun.

"Teacher Wong," said the Captain respectfully. "This is Colonel Thongfa, head of the Chiang Mai crime suppression division. I mentioned to you he'd be dropping by to see you today. He read about your successes: the missing girl, the drug stash. If he's impressed, perhaps—"

"There's no perhaps on the table here," the Colonel cut in. "For some reason I can't work out, we've been given a tub of money for mumbo jumbo psychic consultations. I want nothing to do with it, but I'm under orders. I'm not handing over a single baht unless I'm certain whoever we hire isn't a crook. That could take some time, considering you're all thieves and charlatans. Am I right?"

Samart nodded. "So I hear," he said.

"So, it's down to you to prove your worth."

Samart smiled and adjusted the large yellow chrysanthemum tucked behind his ear.

"Then perhaps you'd be better looking elsewhere," he said.

"What?"

"I'm not in need of money."

"That's not what I heard," said the Colonel.

"And what have you heard, sir?"

"That you peck out a living selling lucky amulets. That you do the odd exorcism and purportedly put clients in touch with their departed loved ones in exchange for food. Doesn't sound like much of a business to me. If you were any good, you'd be rolling in cash. Horse races. Casinos. You could take 'em all. Seems to me you're small fry, Samart, and probably a fraud. You've managed to bamboozle Captain Pairot here and a couple of the other idiots at your local station, but I'm not that green. I'll give you one shot. You've got five minutes to show me what you can do."

"Then I won't waste your time, Colonel."

"Meaning what?"

"I don't have any party tricks for you. I use my gifts for good, not for personal gain. I'm sorry. I can't help you."

The Colonel huffed, fingered his gun, got stiffly to his feet and walked to the door without another word. Captain Pairot shook his head and followed him. The policemen were outside the doorway, putting on their shoes, when Samart called out, "Oh, Pairot. I was sorry to hear about Constable Chalerm. He was a good man."

Pairot looked back briefly at Samart before both officers disappeared into the thick vegetation that surrounded the cabin, separating it from the new 7-Eleven next door. It was clear from his expression that he didn't know what the shaman was talking about. Samart smiled and stretched his aching spine. Cross-legged was never his favourite position. He preferred flat on his back on a mattress. He needed a beer, but he knew the cops would be back sooner or later.

It was sooner.

No more than five minutes had passed before the two officers reappeared in the doorway.

"How did you know?" Colonel Thongfa asked.

"What's that, Colonel?"

"The shooting."

"Somebody got shot?"

Captain Pairot stepped into the room.

"It just this minute came over the police radio in the car. Officer Chalerm stopped a pickup truck out on the Lampang road. Couple of witnesses saw the driver pull a gun, shoot him at point blank range and flee the scene."

"Metallic blue Toyota," said Samart.

"That's right."

"It only happened half an hour ago," said the Colonel, walking into the room without bothering with his shoes. "You couldn't possibly…"

"Lucky guess, then," smiled Samart.

The Archa beer was so cold it sent penguins in icy boots tap dancing over his brain. The mattress was still warm from the sweet smelling skin of Tip, the café singer—his love life, whenever he had money in his purse. And, today, with a five thousand baht advance from the cops, he was flush. A crate of beer. A takeaway papaya salad with sticky rice. An hour with Tip. This was, without question, living.

After today's little performance, Samart had been put on probation as the psychic consultant for the Northern Police Division. The mind of some fool at the police ministry had obviously been turned by all the clairvoyant crime-solvers on cable and decided the Royal Thai Police Force should openly embrace the supernatural. Regional commanders were given a budget and a month to recruit a prophet. Now Samart was, for the unforeseeable future, officially their man in Chiang Mai.

It had all been achieved without a milligram of ability but with plenty of guile and sleight of hand. For twenty years it had been exactly as the Colonel had said. Loser Samart had scratched a living off people's gullibility. He had all the potions, knew all the chants. But he could no more contact the beyond than he could thread a live baby python through his nostril and have it come out his mouth. (He'd seen it on TV and had attempted it himself during one drunken episode in his teens. He'd lost a tonsil in the process.) He'd faked every trick since. All the best-paying customers—those who watched where their money went—weren't taken in by his act. Only the poor, desperate for any grasp of hope, believed in him. He'd been destined to live from hand to mouth for the rest of his worthless life, but then two strokes of good fortune lashed at his lazy buttocks.

His renaissance had begun with a missing girl. Her parents thought she'd been kidnapped, but Samart recognized her from her photo in *Thai Rath*. In fact she'd run away from Bangkok with her Western lover and was holed up in a single room at 103 Condominium. Samart had been called in to perform an exorcism on a haunted lift, and he'd

seen the girl on the roof exercising her Shih Tzu.
Teacher Wong did all the map divining and personal
object caressing. He made a good show of it, and
the sergeant at the Huay Kaew substation was duly
impressed when they found the runaway girl exactly
where Samart had predicted.

Thence followed his first meeting with Captain
Pairot. The officer had come to him as a last resort.
Pairot's unit had raided a Tai Dum heroin plant and
netted fifty kilograms of pure white. But during
the day the dope had vanished from the police
strongroom. The central anti-narcotics commander
was flying up that afternoon to appear in photographs
and pick up the haul. Sadly for Pairot, there would be
nothing to show him. Samart was a gambler. He was
one of a large group of reprobates in a conglomerate
that bet on cockfights and English Premiership
football games. One member of this ring of addicts
was called Nimit, a constable at the Chang Pueak
station to which Pairot was attached. Nimit was in
debt up to his greying temples and wrinkled brow.
He had, on one or two occasions, after the odd
bottle of rice whisky, intimated that one day—yes,
one day soon—he might just help himself to some of
the contraband that passed through his station.

Samart took a gamble, as gamblers do. Perhaps
this was the occasion upon which Nimit had lost his
mind. Samart sat in the empty strongroom, breathed
in the essence of the missing heroin and supposedly

plucked a map reference from thin air. (He'd looked
it up earlier.) It happened to be the home of Nimit,
and the investigating officers found the stash buried
in a plastic ice chest beneath his chicken coop. Samart
was two for two and a minor celebrity in the local
police community. He'd been given rewards for
both finds, and it was evident that there was serious
money to be made from the police if he could just
keep his run of luck going. That's when Colonel
Thongfa heard about him.

Samart decided it wouldn't hurt to give fate a
leg up. Fortunately, there were those who knew
the affairs of the police before the police themselves
heard of them. These were the rescue foundations,
sometimes referred to as the body snatchers. Through
an impressive network of volunteers, short-wave
radios and mobile phones, their members were
invariably first at the scene of an accident or disaster,
natural or otherwise. They were considered to be
charities and were funded by donations, although
it wasn't unknown for the keen young men of the
rescue missions to dip into the odd purse or ease
the victim's breathing by removing a gold necklace.
It wasn't unheard of for one foundation to engage
in public fist fights with another to be first at the
scene.

On that fateful bright March morning when
Colonel Thongfa came to call, Samart had been
connected to his shortwave radio via an earplug

hidden in a large chrysanthemum. He'd been hoping to pick up a traffic accident, a small motorcycle prang with which to impress the officers. But luck had once more perched on his lap. A foundation volunteer had come across the scene of a police killing and was radioing for a rescue truck just as the Colonel and the Captain arrived in the hut. It was perfect timing. Samart's immediate future was gilded, his next month's food bill paid. With his belly full and his brain frozen, he lay back on the peach-perfume-scented mattress and let himself drift. And drift.

He was in the front seat of an old brown Austin A40. Until now he'd always been an observer of his nightmares, a voyeur. He could no sooner have participated than a viewer could step inside a TV and become acquainted with the soap stars. But here in the Austin he could smell the old leather of the upholstery. The semi-headed crone was sitting beside him in the driver's seat. It wasn't her best side. He was surprised to hear his thoughts come out through the mouth of his passenger-seat-self when he said, "What have I done to deserve you?"

"What?" she replied. Drool dribbled from her sluggy black tongue.

"I mean, this is a dream. Am I right? A dream? So why do other men get Lucy Liu in a Catholic high school uniform and I get... if you'll excuse me... road kill?"

She was surprisingly unoffended by his slur.

"You need me, Samart."

"Oh, yeah? And why's that?"

"I'm your spirit guide."

She put a skinny hand on his thigh, and even though he could barely feel it, he squirmed away across the seat.

"I can help you with your career," she went on. "I can pass information on from this side."

"Really? Well, I happen to know from personal experience that all this spirit stuff is bullshit."

"Then what do you think I am?" She leaned closer to him and he could smell some sort of decay, which had obviously been doused with perfume. Her hand moved further up his thigh.

"You're a nightmare."

"Thank you. And you could make me a complete one, Samart."

"How?"

"Invoke me."

"And how would I go about that, as if I couldn't guess?"

Halfhead reached down and pulled both recliner levers, and their seats dropped to the horizontal. Samart clawed at the door but there was no handle. Halfhead rested a hand suddenly as heavy as guilt on his chest. What remained of her face hovered above his. Warm saliva dribbled from her lip as she spoke.

"You just whistle, Samart. Just whistle and I'll do your bidding."

"That's all?"

"And this…"

She pressed her half mouth onto his complete one and snaked her gooey tongue between his lips.

He awoke retching with the taste of stale eel in his throat, the musky scent of rotting flesh in his nostrils. He hurried to the window and dispatched the entire evening's supper into the hibiscus. Nothing would possess him to go back into that nightmare. Nothing. Or so he believed.

For the next month Samart's attachment to the police rapidly came unstuck. It was an unmitigated disaster. He'd hoped to stretch his luck and the odds of chance to two, perhaps three months before they found him out. A premonition here or there gleaned from the body snatchers' network might have bumped him up to four. A nice little nest egg, a retainer buoyed by the odd win bonus, some money put away for rainy days—perhaps even enough for the Amway dealership he'd dreamed of. They made serious money, those Amway reps. But even the averages had turned nasty on poor Samart.

The police had consulted him on eight cases. Bombed, the lot of them. He'd claimed to see the departed spirits of two children who turned up, not at all dead, eating ice cream in the truck of their estranged father. He'd given three grid references for criminal hideouts which turned out to be a temple, a fallow rice paddy and the Lampang governor's summer house. He failed miserably at identifying which of two counter staff at a gold shop had lifted a four karat bracelet, and he picked out the wrong man three times in a lineup, even though all but one were police officers. It was a period of great anguish for the shyster shaman. He put it down to lack of sleep. She'd been there all the time, Halfhead the hag, in his naps and his daydreams, in his nights of floating like a corpse, half-submerged in shallow sleep. She'd been there waiting for her whistle. He'd vowed never to purse his lips again, but a visit from not-only-slightly insane Colonel Thongfa pushed him back into the nightmare world inhabited by the walking sliced.

"You know how many people I've killed?" the policeman asked. It was his opening remark, and it tripped off his tongue as innocently as "Have you had dinner yet?"

"Lots?" Samart offered.

He noticed the senior policeman's hand reach for his pistol. Thongfa was leaning in the doorway. Not point blank range, but he had fifteen rounds, and even if he was an awful shot, one of them could surely splatter Samart over most of the back wall.

"More than lots, witchdoctor Wrong. And, you know? Most of them did nothing to deserve their fate. They didn't make a fool of me. They didn't break my face in front of my superiors in Bangkok.

But I still shot 'em. You want to guess what I'd do to a little fat man with beer breath if he didn't rediscover his supernatural bent in the next twenty-four hours? Go on, Teacher. Guess."

Samart had a good imagination. He didn't need a brochure. So he slept. Six bottles of Archa to the worse, he dived back into his nightmare and let supernature take its course.

"Are you sure it's a good idea to have the press here?" Samart asked, turning to Captain Pairot. The policeman stepped back before the beer fumes could overpower him. Samart was already on his third bottle.

"I thought you'd appreciate the publicity."

"Well, that's just it, isn't it? I won't be getting any. Your colonel's going to take the credit, as usual. Look at him strut."

Samart and Pairot were on the second floor balcony of the police station. It overlooked the car park where Thongfa posed before a large flock of reporters and cameramen. A chain of drowsy monks passed by on the opposite side of the road, ignoring the yapping of an agnostic dog trapped behind a shop-front shutter. It was 6:00 a.m., and the early sun was glinting off the gold *chedi* atop Suthep Mountain. It had been the last vestige of the city's charm. Now it was just another Gomorrah of coloured advertising hoardings held together by concrete. The crowing of cocks had been replaced by the clearing of throats and the hum of breakfast television. In the car park of the Chang Pueak station, the gnarly voice of Colonel Thongfa drowned it all out. He announced that he would be leading a team to apprehend northern Thailand's most wanted man: drug kingpin Khun So. He had reliable information from police intelligence that the villain was staying overnight at a house on the Ping River. Once the compound was secure, the Colonel would allow the press inside to view the catch. Interviews would be acceptable.

"Police intelligence? That's me, right?" Samart slurred.

"Will you relax?" Pairot said with a smile. "You'll be getting more than your fair share once the rewards are divvied up. You should be flattered."

"Because I do all the work and he gets the TV interviews?"

"No, because he trusts you at last."

"Not a great leap of faith. All the tips I've given you for the last two months have been spot on. I'm on a roll. I'm hot stuff. He's not the type to gamble unless he thinks I'm a sure thing. I've earned it."

Samart wasn't exaggerating. Three murders solved. A whole litany of robberies, rapes, riots and rip-offs amicably settled. It had reached the point at police headquarters where most detectives were running their cases by Teacher Wong before wasting their time with an investigation. He saved them a lot of paperwork, yet he was selective. He didn't claim he was able to solve every mystery, even though he could. He didn't want to look too good. It helped his credibility to claim the spirit line was down from time to time. It made his successes all the more remarkable.

This renaissance hadn't come cheaply, of course. Halfhead was there with the answers whenever he needed them. She was a remarkable psychic informant, but he had to pay her in kind. She insisted on a good invoking from time to time. It wasn't the type of thing a living soul could get used to. She was a corpse, after all. There were the flakings, the gas emissions, the joint creaks, the tinkle of fingernails and toenails raining onto the metal floor during great moments of passionate invocation. But even though it all felt unnervingly real, Samart was able to remind himself it was a dream. Just a miserable dip into the subconscious. When he came around, his revulsion at the liaisons in the back seat of the Austin was more than made up for by the superstatus he'd achieved in Chiang Mai. His picture was in magazines. His voice was on the radio. His fake amulets were selling for five thousand baht apiece, and he was well aware he'd soon be independent. He could rid himself of Halfhead and her disgusting wiles. He could assume an inscrutable cloak of mystery and make a living selling black magic memorabilia and Amway products. The future was looking rosy.

But then the flock of seagulls hit the jet engine.

With a company of media representatives established under the shade of a duck heel tree, Thongfa's commandos scaled the walls of the compound like Special Olympic ninjas. Some made it to the top, unsure of what to do once there. Most made it halfway up the ropes and then slid back down, blowing into their palms to assuage the burning sensation. Some lost their grip completely and thudded into the bougainvilleas. Only one brave soul made it over the wall and into the compound. He unlatched the gate from the inside, and Thongfa and his men advanced along the gravel driveway, making enough noise to raise the dead.

Samart was alone in the front seat of the Austin A40. He had a beer bottle in his hand. Not knowing why he was there, and for want of something to do, he sipped at the drink. It was flat. No, not flat, tasteless. Totally without… texture. It was as if he were pouring merely the concept of beer into his mouth, without experiencing any of the pleasures. This should have been a dream, but it was different. He was real. Even if the beer was non-existentially awful, and the car interior was a set from a long-running season of nightmares, he had substance. Something had happened. He considered briefly that he might have been elevated to a higher spiritual plain—been awarded a karmic gold star by the gods. But, of course, that was unlikely. There were mornings he couldn't even elevate himself out of bed.

The view outside the Austin was like traveling through country lanes at warp speed. It looked like a nice day. There was nobody in the driver's seat and the steering wheel spun both clockwise and anti-clockwise like a prop on a children's carousel. There was a dead jasmine lei hanging forlornly from the rear-view mirror. Always bad luck to have anything dead in a motor vehicle. But as he was untangling it, the mirror shifted position and in the glass he saw the probably smiling face of Halfhead. There was something different about her. She seemed to have picked up another dimension since he'd last seen her. She was wearing a newly bloodied frock with a white lace collar. There was lipstick on her half lips.

"Something bad's happened," he said. His voice resonated unexpectedly around the interior of the car, vibrating the spring-headed basset hound on the back window ledge.

"This isn't a dream anymore," she said.

"You're real now?"

"No."

"Then?"

"You aren't."

"So, I'm…"

"Dead."

Without provocation she reached forward and slapped his ear. It hurt.

"I felt that."

"You'll be feeling a lot worse."

"What? Why?"

A genuine fear was rising from the rusty bed of the Austin and gnawing at his ankles. It was as if he'd driven over the carcass of Terror somewhere back on the road, and its entrails had wrapped themselves around the axles and were seeping in through the bolt holes. He wasn't the driver, but he felt responsible for its mutilation.

"I'm having a very bad dream," he said, and instantly knew he wasn't.

"You're about to," she said, and all at once she was beside him behind the wheel. "A very bad dream from which you'll never awaken. A nightmare that will stick to you like poison ivy."

"I don't…"

"Tsk! That stain's going to be hard to get out. You should have soaked it straightaway. Men never get that concept."

He had no idea what she was talking about until he followed her gaze to the large blood-framed hole in his lower chest. He hadn't noticed it. The wound was like a centrifugal fun fair painting on the white canvas of his silk shirt.

"I am dead," he said.

"It happens."

"How?"

"Insane Colonel Thongfa. He'd just raided the house you informed him of. It belonged to one the many mistresses of somebody so important no news channel dared mention his name. And that unmentionable somebody just happened to be in bed beside her at the time. The Colonel barely had time to shoot you before he vanished from public life."

"But…"

Samart was fussing with his chest wound, attempting to gather the edges of his shirt together to hide the offal.

"But you told me Khun So would be there," he reminded her. "You said…"

"Sorry."

"You knew whose house that was."

She smiled, and her sluggy tongue unfurled to her Adam's apple.

"But you're my spirit guide," he said, his voice several octaves above masculine.

She put her hand on his knee.

"You know?" she said. "I might have exaggerated about my role in your universe just a bit."

"Then I don't get it. What are you?"

"Just a regular old malevolent spirit. A nasty ghost with a chip on her shoulder."

"Against me?"

"Yes."

"What have I ever done to you?"

"Lottery numbers."

"What about lottery numbers?"

"You made them up."

"Of course I made them up."

He started to laugh and his spleen slipped out onto his lap. He opened the glove box hoping to find something to patch the hole. It was annoying. He ripped the registration sticker off the windshield, but the gum no longer stuck. He threw it down in a rage.

"All this is because I gave you bum lottery numbers?"

"It certainly wasn't the worst thing you did. You were lying to people for years about serious things. Pretending to talk to relatives on this side. Having the mourning ones hand over their valuables. Giving them false hope. You've pissed off a lot of folk, Samart. A lot of lost souls are dying to meet you. We have a little admiration society. We Buddhists may not have a heaven, Teacher Wong, but we have a nice selection of hells. We're on our way to one I think you'll enjoy."

The scene beyond the windows had passed quickly through purple dusk to a mauve-black night. The only lights beside the road came from bushes burning. The car began to slow and figures stepped out from behind the bonfires. It occurred to Samart that whoever researched for the *Living Dead* movies had done a field trip to purgatory because zombies really did look like that. Some of them made Halfhead seem positively pretty. They laboured painfully toward the car as it rolled to a stop.

"Look," Samart said, holding back his panic, "I want to lodge an appeal. I get sent to hell because I got the lottery numbers wrong? That's ridiculous, and it's not fair. I was just starting to make something of myself."

"Based on lies, Samart. As always. Do you really think it doesn't matter? People came to you out of desperation. They wanted help. My husband was a security guard. He got laid off during the recession. He was depressed. He turned to drink. Our poor but happy life was disintegrating. My neighbour told me you had a gift. I came to you and…"

"I know you?"

"You probably don't remember me. I've let myself go a bit since then. I told you about our problem. I gave you a sack of rice and my mother's ring and you gave me the lottery numbers. I asked if you were sure. You were confident. You said you'd seen the numbers in a dream, but you couldn't be certain what order they would appear in. I believed in you. I put all the savings I'd hidden away from my husband, sold our fruit handcart, borrowed money from friends and bought every ticket—every combination of those numbers. Every ticket I could find from one side of the city to the other. And the lottery numbers were announced, and not one of your numbers came up. Not one, Samart. Now what are the odds of that? There should be a prize for having no numbers, don't you think?"

"It's a gamble. You can't blame—"

He was interrupted by the clawing of blackened fingernails against the windows. To his horror, Halfhead started to wind down the glass.

"Well, I do," she said. "You gave me your word and I believed you. My husband was sober when I told him I'd lost all our money. He smiled and walked out. When he came back a few hours later with the machete, he was drunk. I don't know where he'd found the booze. We had no cash. He's a strong man. It only took one blow to do this. Impressive, isn't it? Split down the middle like a coconut. I didn't feel a thing. Not until I got here. Then the hurt and resentment began."

"I didn't…"

"Yes, you did. And you deserve whatever's coming to you. You'll have an awful time here, Samart. My job's done. I'll eventually move on to somewhere with better décor, but you've accrued so much bad debt, you'll be here for a very long time. You'll have an age to meet all those spirits you claimed to be talking to when you were back there. And you'd be surprised how many of us gals are still in need of a good invoking from time to time.

You're going to have your work cut out for you, Teacher Wong."

Icy hands reached in through the window and caressed the petrified shaman, lifted his shirt, pinched at his soft flesh. His eyes were red even without the benefit of makeup. His heart was full and heavy as lard and sliding gradually down to the hole in his front. Tears rolled down his cheeks as he imagined his future. A miserable future without end. And as if all that weren't bad enough… the beer was crap.

Colin Cotterill

Colin Cotterill was born in London and trained as a teacher and set off on a world tour that didn't ever come to an end. Colin has taught and trained teachers in Thailand and on the Burmese border. He spent several years in Laos, initially with UNESCO and wrote and produced a forty-program language teaching series; *English By Accident*, for Thai national television.

All the while, Colin continued with his two other passions; cartooning and writing. He contributed regular columns for the *Bangkok Post*. It wasn't until his work with trafficked children that he found himself sufficiently stimulated to put together his first novel, *The Night Bastard* (Suk's Editions. 2000). The reaction to that first attempt was so positive that Colin decided to take time off and write full-time.

Since 1990, Colin has been a regular cartoonist for national publications. A Thai language translation of his cartoon scrapbook, *Ethel and Joan Go to Phuket* and weekly social cartoons in *The Nation* newspaper. In 2004, an illustrated bilingual column '*cycle logical*' was launched in Matichon Weekly magazine. Later, both comic strips have been published in book form.

In 2009, Colin Cotterill received the Crime Writers Association Dagger in the Library award for being "the author of crime fiction whose work is currently giving the greatest enjoyment to library users."

Dolphins Inc.

Christopher G. Moore

1.0

Where are you?

Queen Sirikit Center, Bangkok, Thailand

Inside one of the smaller conference rooms, the air-conditioning blasting multiple streams over the audience. In the back a youngish Thai man—just out of his teens—his hair short, as if he'd recently disrobed as a monk or left military service. But he didn't seem like the type for either the monkhood or the army. Chinapat had the soft, nerdy look of a man-boy slumped before a computer screen as a way of life.

He sat in quiet serenity, either meditating or somewhere online inside his skull, slowly rubbing his hands, moving his fingers together as if the meat locker chill temperature had seeped deep into his body or he had lost his concentration, hand on the mouse, the cursor frozen on the screen. Dressed in a suit and tie, and cheap black shoes from the Sunday market, the kind with thick rubber soles. Such shoes allowed Chinapat, like a phantom, silently and without notice, to disappear inside a room.

Inside the frigid room was the object of Chinapat's first professional job.

A middle-aged Japanese man in dark glasses looked him over the way a father looks over a son, part pride, part doubt and disapproval, as if his expectations had been exceeded and dashed at the same time. The Japanese man showed him a photograph of Tanaka.

"Eliminate him," he said.

Chinapat glanced at the podium. Mr. Tanaka, a representative of an obscure but well-financed Japanese film distributor, spoke to the early morning symposium. It was Friday at 8:30 a.m. Chinapat couldn't remember the last time he'd been awake at 8:30 in the morning; no memory came back.

He watched as Mr. Tanaka began to read from his notes, looking up at a thin audience of no more than seventy-five people—a scattering of journalists, film students, some representatives from the Japanese embassy and the Ministry of Foreign Affairs, and a few walk-ins who had read about the event in the *Bangkok Post*. Most of the audience had blue lips from the cold. They'd been paid a handsome sum to wrap themselves in coats and scarves to survive the arctic blast from the ventilation system. The first two rows of hard-looking Japanese men, with thick necks sticking like redwoods from their white shirts and dark suits, sat so still they looked like sculptures. Chinapat sighed, thinking as he examined the men in the first rows that he'd signed onto a very long payroll.

Mr. Tanaka had a thin moustache and gleaming teeth that looked artificial—hard, resilient objects that would outlive the man by centuries. The speaker appeared more Chinese than Japanese with his round face and large eyes. Chinapat wondered if this was the result of a deep flaw as Tanaka lowered his glasses, looked up from his notes and nodded at one of the men in the first row. Tanaka's unsmiling stone-like face surveyed the audience. He spoke in English, his tone reserved and serious. Chinapat wondered what it was like to actually kill a man in the real world. And, in particular, what it would feel like to kill Tanaka.

"We resist outsiders who don't know our history," Tanaka said, looking at the audience. "Such people do not respect or honor our way of life, our traditions. Our history, like your history in Thailand, is both noble and ancient. Outsiders would try to destroy our culture. We have terrorists like the *Sea Shepherd*, saying that because we hunt limited numbers of dolphins and pilot whales we are wrong. How can that be?" Tanaka shrugged his shoulders, looking out at his audience. "How can the Japanese way of life be wrong? It's not logical. It's not scientific."

Chinapat thought the speech sounded like something from the lips of an old analogue way of viewing reality. He opened one eye and glanced down at his watch before he closed them again. Waiting was the worst part of his job. Listening to a speech from Tanaka was the second worst part. He quite enjoyed, though, the planning, working out the details—place, time and, most important of all, the exit from the scene once the work was done.

Mr. Tanaka hadn't made his first job easy. In the real world there were no "cheat codes" to game the system. He had to figure out stuff one step at a time. Tanaka hadn't stayed in any of the luxury hotels on Sukhumvit Road. Instead he had holed up, as if expecting trouble, in a compound in Thonglor— the heart of the Japanese expat community—ringed with CCTV cameras, security personnel and limited access. On screen, none of these obstacles would have taken more than a few keystrokes to blow through.

Tanaka droned on in a public speech fashion— all words, no images—with lots of very important people in the audience who actually appeared to be listening. Chinapat hated all of those words, and he hated more how the words made him captive, a passive, helpless, patient observer. Analogue boredom flowed like pain throughout the system.

The overhead lights dimmed, and behind him the film started.

The screening of *The Taiji Truth* ended with a slow fade to a group of fishermen sitting together with their wives and children. The villagers lived in Taiji, located in southwestern Japan. These were the same people who'd done the heavy work, the slicing and cutting, the killing in *The Cove*. In this film the fishermen appeared as heroes, dressed like samurai. They talked about the history of their village and its simple, honest people, who only wanted to continue the traditions of their ancestors. Self-sufficient, modest, proud and very Japanese... but no one was talking about Academy Awards. The film had been financed by members of the far right in Japan and had been taken to Asian countries to show the true story of the people of Taiji and their relationship with the annual dolphin hunt.

The camera floated across the faces, making them look like humble, salt of the earth villagers who had little in terms of material possessions. The kind of people one rarely thought about as living in Japan. Chinapat thought they looked like men, women and children from a village near the Laotian border he'd once visited just to see what such a place looked like. He was more careful about unstructured visits, as they often led to little more than dust, barking dogs, chickens scratching the ground and the smell of wood fires. Bangkok was different. So was Taiji.

No more than five minutes into the documentary, there was a jump cut. Nothing gracefully prepared the audience for what came next.

A shudder arose as the screen filled with the Taiji bay boiled up a gruesome red. Blood gushed from dozens of gutted dolphins as local Japanese villagers slaughtered as if on a battleground, hacking and stabbing and cutting through the flesh. Tanaka started shouting in Japanese. A couple of the men in the first row ran to the front, using their sizeable bodies to block the screen. Other Japanese men from the second row ran to the projection room in the back. Chinapat heard them cursing in Japanese.

"Ladies and gentlemen, we have had someone sabotage our film. Those who hate Japan stop at nothing to hurt us. What you are seeing is an example of the history of Anglo–Saxon cultural imperialism. They seek to interfere and bring down our traditions. We will stand together against such people."

The Japanese in the audience applauded. After a few seconds they were on their feet giving Tanaka a standing ovation. It was Tanaka's moment of glory. He actually smiled and bowed to the audience. The men outside the projection room were having difficulty getting in. The projectionist had locked the door from the inside.

"In Japan we follow the principle of sustainable use. Dolphins are a renewable resource."

Chinapat kept his eye on the stage, watching the sea of dead and dying dolphins dancing over the faces and chests of the Japanese men from the audience who stood shoulder to shoulder, as if they'd practiced this formation. The shallow inland bay reminded him of Fanta strawberry red, one of Chinapat's favorite drinks as a boy. The rest of the audience reacted with confusion and anger. Watching the men from the first five minutes gleefully slaughtering the dolphins horrified the women in the audience. They registered a common emotion, which exploded like a flock of birds that had spotted an eagle circling. The roaring sound of stale breath sucked deep back into the lungs, a rising tone of disgust salted with despair.

Finally the film stopped, and the men who'd been blocking the screen filed back and took their seats. Three other men came out of the projection booth, leaving a comrade inside to keep an eye on the projectionist.

As Tanaka resumed his speech, apologizing for the interruption and promising to file a complaint, he said, "What you've just seen is the work of terrorists."

More applause burst from a sizeable section of the audience. Chinapat observed that a number of those applauding were missing little fingers. The absent appendage didn't muffle or reduce the sound of the clapping. Then an attractive young Thai woman with red streaks in her long black hair entered from one of the side doors—she looked no more than seventeen or eighteen. She wore a tight, short black miniskirt and a crisp white cotton blouse with shiny buttons that looked like military decorations. She walked straight to his row and sat in the seat next to him. "I know who you are," she said. "And I have a message for you."

He didn't recognize her at first. "You've mistaken me for someone else, younger sister," he said.

"It's a trap," she said, looking straight ahead at the stage. "We've been set up."

"That's not my reading," he said.

Her name was Seven and she'd expected an argument. "That's because your calculations are off point four," she said.

He ran through the sequence from top to bottom. "Fuck, you're right," he said, his mouth ajar. "How did that happen?"

She leaned over and whispered, "You were in a hurry. Now we don't have much time. But I have a backup plan."

One of the things Chinapat loved most about Seven was that she always came with a fully developed contingency program.

She firmly grabbed his hand, and together they moved down the row to the exit door and out into the main lobby. Seven handed him a shopping bag and pointed to the men's restroom. A couple of minutes later, Chinapat emerged wearing a baseball cap, dark glasses, Wrangler jeans and a T-shirt with a small dolphin icon above the heart.

2.0

Where are you?

Nana Entertainment Plaza

In a small, overcrowded back room of a bar converted into an office, a couple of tables, chairs, bookcases, a filing cabinet and two enormous safes occupied the area behind a locked set of teak doors.

Sitting amid gray smoke, a heavy-set Middle-Eastern man named Jaul slumped in front of a computer screen. His enormous stomach rose above the edge of the table as his right hand moved the mouse and his left hand fed a large, freshly fried chicken drumstick into his mouth. Jaul was online, working through a pirated version of an early program of an archeological dig outside Baghdad. He was the owner of the Smoke but No Fire Bar.

The bar, once a travel agency, was discreetly set back from the staircase on the second floor of the Nana Entertainment Plaza. It was early morning, and the plaza was deserted. A few delivery trucks downstairs. Otherwise only a stray cat and a couple of resident dogs occupied the narrow corridors. Jaul loved the early morning, when he was left alone to count his money. His was a popular bar, and his women tall and young and beautiful. Money, piles of cash, accumulated every night like clockwork.

He had counted his money twice and made notes in a ledger. Behind the chair where he sat, the safe door was ajar. Through the door appeared rows of stacked Thai thousand and five hundred baht notes.

One of Seven's cyber friends had struck up a friendship with Pepsi, who worked at Jaul's Smoke but No Fire Bar in Nana. Pepsi was a dancer and she took drugs. She paid cash for some cyber work involving several foreign customers, and Seven had been a subcontractor in refining Pepsi's network of clients. Like most addicts Pepsi had a keen awareness of where lots of money was hidden and loved to gossip. She traded information about Jaul's safe after Seven promised a full system upgrade and payment security that her bookie couldn't hack.

Chinapat stepped into Jaul's office, finding crude, out-of-date furniture and equipment. The primitive quality of Jaul's software made his computer system no better than a toy. A porn site with several naked actors on a sofa flickered on the computer screen.

"What do you want?" Jaul asked, looking at Chinapat and then at Seven. "A job?"

There was a twinkle in his eye as he mentally undressed Seven.

"Don't do that," she said.

Jaul understood exactly what she meant. "Pray tell me your wish."

"The money," Seven said. He followed her eyes to the open safe door. Pimping clearly was more lucrative than murder.

As Jaul swung around to close the safe, Chinapat caught him along the side of the head with a 9mm Glock. There was nothing like hardened plastic to send a man to dreamland. A gush of blood dribbled down Jaul's cheek. His attempt to fall back over his keyboard was interrupted by the bulge of his stomach, leaving him in the no-man's land of being half-suspended in space. "Someone named Jaul should make better choices," said Chinapat.

Seven rolled her eyes, knowing that Chinapat had accessed the Arabic dictionary as he stuffed the 9mm into the waistband of his jeans.

They cleaned out the safe, stuffing Seven's suitcase with over a million baht. Jaul remained unconscious as Chinapat left first, carrying the suitcase. A moment later Seven followed.

At the Nana and Sukhumvit Road intersection, beside the police traffic control box on the corner, they met and climbed into a taxi. "How do you know this isn't another trap?" Chinapat asked.

Seven held the suitcase on her lap. "Soon the Japanese will be looking for you."

He knew there was no going back to Queen Sirikit Center. "Do we have enough money?"

Seven nodded her head. "For the startup, yes. Then we'll need financing. Worry about that later."

Not only had she saved Chinapat from falling into a trap laid by the Japanese, but she had the most calming effect when it came to assigning worry to a future to-do list. He could love a woman like that.

3.0

Where are you?

Bangkok Port

Located at the mouth of the Chao Phraya River, Bangkok Port—people also called it the Port of Klong Toey—had been a trading hub since the ninth century. A lot of sailors, pirates, traders, merchants and adventurers had walked the docks. As the taxi pulled to a stop, the sky was dotted with large cranes like columns of dinosaur skeletons erected up and down the shoreline of the Chao Phraya. Beyond the cranes were cargo ships, rice barges and fishing ships at anchor. Waiting.

Wires from Seven's cell phone ended inside her ears. She talked as they walked down the road. Chinapat shifted the suitcase from one hand to the other. Real cash had a certain heft; the weight of money, though, never seemed heavy. They walked for fifteen minutes, and the sun was overhead and hot. Sweat rolled down Chinapat's face, but Seven's skin was cool and untouched by a single drop of perspiration. That's when they saw a skinny white-haired *farang* man with a broad smile, waving, in the distance. As they came closer, the man could have passed for late forties to early seventies. He introduced himself as Mr. Shockley and led them up the gangplank of the ship with "DOLPHIN SHEPHERD" stenciled on the bow.

"Welcome, partners," Shockley said. "Let me show you around."

First stop, and his point of pride, was a crane equipped with a large metal claw—a giant version of the fairground arcade game. Chinapat exchanged a look with Seven.

"Are you the owner?" asked Chinapat, frowning under his baseball cap.

"I am authorized to act on behalf of the owners," he said. "As chunks of ice shelves calf into the Antarctic, we bring the ship alongside and harvest the purest drinking water on the planet. Australia is running out of fresh, pure water. So is Japan. The future of water is locked in icebergs."

"How do you drink an iceberg?" asked Chinapat.

"You bottle it," Shockley said.

Seven took the suitcase from Chinapat and handed Jaul's pimping money over to Shockley. "Aren't you going to count it?" she asked.

"No need," he said.

"Now that we are partners, shouldn't we know who our partners are?" Seven asked, wondering if this was the first time that brothel money had been laundered through an iceberg business.

"Yeah, that's right," said Chinapat. "Partners shouldn't have secrets from each other."

Shockley had hoped they would have taken more interest in the machinery, the engineering work that had gone into the crane, and shown some curiosity about where the ice was stored on board and how it was transferred to the bottling plants. He loved telling others stories of the early days of trial and error, testing, equipment breakdowns and violent storms at sea, where it was like riding an eighteen-story building struggling sideways over forty-foot waves. He led them to a stateroom and sat them at a conference table. There was a huge computer screen, and Shockley clicked the mouse to fill the screen with what looked familiar to Chinapat. A fishing village in a small bay.

"That's a village in Japan. It's Taiji," said Chinapat.

"Our new bottling plant will be located here," he said, directing a cursor to a point near the village center. "We will employ most of the able-bodied men in the village."

"Who is 'we'?" asked Seven.

The problem with the word "we," she thought, is that the edges break off when it comes to describing the merger of intelligences that include human interfaces. Unscrambling the nodes and networks is a messy business.

Shockley scratched his chin and smiled. "The original settlers of the Antarctic," he said, looking at the two new partners and trying to read their reaction. "Those who know the icebergs better than anyone."

"Dolphins," said Chinapat. "We're back to dolphins again."

"We are returning to the sea," said Seven with a smile.

"The water inside icebergs is thousands of years old. Some icebergs have drinking water older than man," said Shockley. "There is no man-made tradition older than iceberg water. We have approached the Taiji people, who have agreed to give up killing dolphins for harvesting pure water. The new harvest carries the dignity of the past, and it is the past they worship."

As the *Dolphin Shepherd* sailed from Bangkok Port, Chinapat caught a glimpse of the two rows of Japanese men with long swords and megaphones shouting slogans as they ran along the docks, waving and shouting, and Jaul waddled behind, trying to keep up. He looked like an old walrus, shaking his ham-sized flipper and barking. Bringing up the rear were hundreds of Nana Plaza bar girls. As they set sail, Chinapat grasped the railing with both hands. Seven stood beside him. They watched as the women gutted and slaughtered the black-suited men, turning the Chao Phraya River red. The swords dissolved in the hands of the Japanese. The megaphones fell silent. By the time they reached the sea, the water was again clean and pure.

Bangkok Port soon was a tiny rim on the horizon. Shockley produced a device the size of a cell phone, running his fingers across a small screen until it lit up. He offered the device to Seven. "It's the owners. They want to communicate directly."

She held the device close to her ear and smiled. Then she handed it to Chinapat, who pressed it against his ear, a big smile crossing his face. It was somewhere between the rush of the sound from a large seashell, running water and music coming from a thousand crystal glasses, each filled with different levels of water. The background songs registered from deep inside the electromagnetic spectrum.

4.0

Where are you?

Chinapat: Still at Dolphin Shepherd, Simulation 28478, GENESIS 32 Vector

Where are you?

Seven: Meet you at Login node loading hydrogen atoms to emit microwaves at the

frequency "21-centimetre line" sequencing
EXODUS 4:24-26 router

4.1

Where are you?

Queen Sirikit Center, Bangkok, Thailand

Inside one of the smaller conference rooms, the air-conditioning blasting multiple streams over the audience. In the back sat a youngish Asian woman—still in her teens, her hair long and dyed red in streaks. The young woman was dressed in the white pressed cotton blouse and black short skirt of a university student. The too tight skirt just fit inside the outer perimeters for a certified conservative sexual university outfit found in Bangkok. The Gucci handbag also fit. The .38 Smith and Wesson inside the handbag was non-standard university issue. Seven had the confident and alert look of a woman-girl whose attention floated across the room, perching, sensing, flying off to another perch, constantly on the move.

Seven could never sit in quiet serenity like Chinapat. That was his problem. All that meditating had over-focused his attention on one thing. For example, she thought he'd complain of the tropical heat inside the room. The temperature was like a sauna. Many in the audience had wilted like unwatered flowers.

Inside the hotbed was the object of Seven's first professional job.

A middle-aged Japanese woman in dark glasses, old enough to be her mother, had sat with her in the back of a BMW. Looking her over the way a mother looks over a daughter before a first date—part pride, part doubt and disapproval, as if her expectations had been exceeded and dashed at the same time—the Japanese woman had showed her a photograph of a woman named Tanaka. She was an activist filmmaker, and she had drawn an audience of activists, artists, journalists and NGOs to hear her speak about her dolphin film documentary, showing a terrible, cruel slaughter.

In the parking lot a couple of dozen Japanese men in dark suits used threats to stop people from going inside. Only a few people were intimidated enough to leave. The others filed past the Japanese men with tattooed necks and missing small fingers.

"Eliminate Tanaka," the Japanese woman in the car had said.

Even though Seven hadn't asked why the activist was scheduled for removal, the middle-aged Japanese woman felt obligated to give a reason. "She's a troublemaker."

Chinapat slipped into the seat next to Seven and whispered, "It's a trap."

Seven smiled, glancing over at him, squeezing his knee. "I have the cheat code."

He frowned, pretending to be above easy shortcuts. Chinapat had a cheat code to get out of virtual prison, but only if nothing else in his source code kit worked. Cheaters ran up the white flag of surrender before experiencing any real degree of panic or desperation or being black-boxed and cut into pixels. He never thought of Seven as a cheater. Before he could object, the large screen behind Tanaka filled with a video of dolphins churning in blood red waters. The volume of their high-pitched squeals rolled through the room, echoing off the walls, ceiling and floor.

Seven leaned down and rummaged inside her handbag until her hand emerged gripping a .38 Smith and Wesson. She rested it on her lap, looking straight ahead. As she began to rise from her seat, two men from the row of seats behind her grabbed her arms. The gun dropped on the floor. The sonar whelp of the dolphins murdered on screen masked the sound of the gun hitting the floor.

4.2

Where are you?

Below deck, Dolphin Shepherd

As far as Seven could see, she was surrounded by mountains of shaved ice. From the port side, she wiped icy fog from the window pane and looked out at the calm blue sea. A ridge of white foam passed beside the ship. She shivered, moving from side to side, but nothing seemed to bring warmth. The ice had gone straight into her blood, lungs and brain. She sat in a corner, arms folded around her chest. She'd never seen so much ice in a room.

The bulkhead door opened and Shockley stepped inside, closing the door behind him. He wore a hat, mufflers and a heavy coat. Unwrapping the scarf from around his neck took several minutes. When he finished, he handed it to Seven, who looked up with a smile.

"Using an old cheat code to game the system," he said, slowly shaking head.

Seven took the scarf and cocooned herself like a larva. "How long do I have to stay here?" she said, sighing.

"Until you earn their trust," said Shockley. "And that won't be easy, given your last jump. But they have all the time in the world."

"Chinapat?" she whimpered.

"He's harvesting pure water from our iceberg factory. The dolphins trust your friend," said Shockley.

"Can't you release me to Chinapat?"

Shockley smiled. "No one is stopping him from coming for you."

Seven blinked, only her wet eyes visible through a slit in the scarf. Hot tears froze halfway down her cheek as she wondered if Chinapat had left her behind, jumping to the next router. She hung her head. On all sides heaps of pure ice thousands of years old seemed to grow, crowding her into a small corner. Her arms wrapped around her raised knees, she rocked back and forth. "When will he come?"

4.3

Where are you?

The Cove, Taiji, Japan

Chinapat sat alone on the long sandy beach, facing the sea and the *Dolphin Shepherd*, anchored in the harbor. Small skiffs ferried ice from the ship to the shore. The cranes on the ship loaded ice onto skiffs. The clear sea surrounding the ship boiled with dolphins, jumping and diving, swimming alongside the skiffs and guiding them to docks that dotted the shore.

Seven started to run as she saw him in the distance. His large head and broad shoulders were unmistakable against an almond sky. She sprinted the last thirty meters, feeling the warm sand between her toes. Shockley's scarf trailed behind her until at last it fell from her, leaving a long silk wound in the sand.

Reaching Chinapat, she fell on her knees next to him.

He took her hand, not taking his eyes off the *Dolphin Shepherd* and the skiffs.

"I told you it was a trap," he said.

"The Sim felt so real," she said. "The ice, the cold. Shockley. The scarf."

He turned his head, looking at her eyes for a moment and then behind her. "But it was real." The scarf had turned into a scarlet red river in the sand, gurgling as it flowed toward the sea. Baby dolphins dropped one by one, as if from an assembly line, into the sea. They both watched as the cove teamed with dolphins.

"The scarf was from you," she said. "You trusted me."

He shrugged. Chinapat had never thought of giving another person a cheat code for release from virtual prison reality. He had only one. Once it had been used, that was the end of it. There was no second code. If things went wrong now, he'd remain in a limbo with no hope of escape. It wasn't necessary to tell Seven the obvious consequences of his decision to help her.

"We are going back home?" she asked. Chinapat smiled, knowing that her idea of home was far away from the dolphin world.

He nodded his head. "We're not finished. Tonight we sail for Bangkok on the *Dolphin Shepherd*. This time we can't make any stupid mistakes. We play by the rules."

"But I played by the noir subset of rules," she said, a tone of anger creeping into her voice. "It is permissible."

Seven was a literalist. And she believed in free will. Bangkok, the epicenter of noir, had enticed her to take any contract and take any risk. She'd ignored that the underlying source code for intelligence and purity perimeter violations established a deterministic but chaotic system not bound by entropy. But the old assumptions died hard. Bottom line was that no free will patches could be deployed to destroy predetermined outcomes. Emerging intelligent systems and water source purity were jointly linked and encoded with a level-eight firewall, which even the best cheat codes couldn't breach. They returned to Bangkok, not as observers, but as partisans taking their place inside a deterministic noir world where their mission had already been predetermined.

Once Seven reviewed and uploaded the operative conditions, she'd understand that her feelings of pain, pleasure and emotions were real. Her problem arose from the perception of freedom and liberty, which felt also overwhelmingly real. In fact they were illusions in the system where the fundamental unreality was hidden at the quantum level. These mental conditions were bought and sold through administrator level cheat codes. Seven believed freedom and liberty were a natural right. It was a common mistake.

The question in Chinapat's mind was whether she'd learnt her lesson.

Chinapat would find out the answer in Bangkok on a stormy night when the Japanese mafia came to greet the arrival of the *Dolphin Shepherd* at the Port of Klong Toey. They stood under umbrellas in the rain waiting for the ship. Armed men with swords and guns would take a stand, one consistent with their huge appetite for dolphin meat. Icebergs, no matter how pure, were no substitute for that sensation of pleasure.

"What do they expect?" Seven asked as the *Dolphin Shepherd* left the cove.

"They will offer you another contract," said Chinapat.

"Am I free to accept their offer?" she asked.

Shockley joined them on the foredeck. He handed Seven a glass of pure iceberg water. "Ten thousand years ago, this water froze into ice. Today it is water again. When was it free? As ice? As water?"

"Water just is. How can water or ice be free?" She looked troubled. "Am I free to upload to home base?"

Shockley turned to Chinapat. "She is free to drink the iceberg water. Ten thousand years a sip. Once you've swallowed and digested the water time, you can phase back. Meanwhile, you'll have another offer to consider."

5.0

Where are you?

Chinapat: Cross-check Highway, Chon Buri Province 28480, ALPHA 16 Vector

Where are you?

Seven: Meet you at Login node loading hydrogen atoms to emit microwaves at the frequency "091-centimetre line" sequencing OMEGA 7:33-39 router

5.1

Where are you?

Highway No. 41 between Kms 6 and 7, Muang District

Several hours had passed since the *Dolphin Shepherd* had docked at the Port of Klong Toey, and Chinapat guided Seven through a scrub of Japanese gangsters in their black suits and ties. The gangsters blocked their path, wielding swords and guns, threatening and shouting, demanding and gesturing. Shockley watched as Chinapat found the keys for the Honda 500 motorcycle. Seven sat on the back and Chinapat slowly found a path through the gangsters. Twenty minutes later, Chinapat pulled behind a gray-bronze van. They were on the way to Chon Buri.

"That's the van," said Seven.

Chinapat followed behind at a safe distance and at Kilometer 6 pulled ahead and cut in front of the van. The driver honked angrily and tried to pass him. As Chinapat pulled alongside, Seven had extended her arms, both hands clutched together, pointing a .38 Smith and Wesson at the driver. She waved for him to pull to the curb. The driver said something to the passenger in the seat next to him and, before Kilometer 7 was reached, pulled to a stop on the shoulder of the highway.

Seven kept the gun pointed at the men in the van.

"Get out of the van. Hands up," said Chinapat.

"Do you know who our patron is?" asked the van driver.

"Shut up and open the back," said Chinapat.

The driver clutched his fists and stepped forward, arm cocked and ready to swing.

Seven fired a round over his head. "He said open the fucking van."

When the door opened, inside the modified van were three large dolphins.

Just as Shockley had said, in the back two female Indo-Pacific humpback dolphins and one male lay under a green plastic sheet. Chinapat pulled the sheet away, exposing the pregnant female on a rubber mattress. The dolphins from the cove at Taiji had passed along the kidnapping alert minutes after the gang caught the dolphins in the sea near Trang. The kidnappers were on their way to deliver the dolphins to a powerful person in Chon Buri province.

The police arrived minutes after Seven phoned. They looked at the dolphins as the men in the van watched.

"Do you know who our patron is?" the driver asked one of the cops.

"You're under arrest," said the head policeman. He turned to Seven. "You've been a great help. We will handle it from here."

"What will you do?" asked Chinapat.

"Of course, in time, we will return the dolphins to the sea," the policeman said.

Seven, at last, could understand the dolphins communicating in the van. They were saying that they hadn't much time remaining, and soon it would be too late.

"There isn't much time," Seven said to the cop.

The gangsters, who'd been silent, looked at each other and then at Chinapat and Seven. "You have no choice but to let us go," said the leader. "You will regret this. Hey, what are you doing?"

Chinapat had climbed into the van and Seven joined him. He rolled down the window. "We will release them." He didn't wait for an answer. The police and gangsters stood on the road, watching as Chinapat squealed the tires, kicking up gravel, as he drove the van back onto the highway.

5.2

Where are you?

Beach, Muang District, Chon Buri

Chinapat pushed the accelerator to the floor as the van sped toward the sea. He cut off the highway, and the van bumped along a gravel road. They could both smell the sea. The dolphins, despite their weakened condition, had continued to sing during the entire journey. The rescue revived their spirits. When the van reached the end of a dirt road, Seven got out of the van and guided Chinapat as he backed onto the beach, the surf lapping at the rear wheels.

Seven spotted the *Dolphin Shepherd* a couple of hundred meters offshore. Shockley and four men worked the oars on the rowboat. Landing the boat, Shockley and his men ran up the beach, and within minutes they had carried the first female out of the van and laid her on the sand. Not long afterward, the other two dolphins were lined up on the beach, too. Shockley's men removed two cases of iceberg water from the rowboat. Shockley opened several bottles and poured the cool water over the three dolphins. One by one, the dolphins slipped away.

Police sirens wailed in the distance as Shockley and his men climbed back into the rowboat. "That will be the police. You'd better come with us," he said.

Seven shook her head. She squeezed Chinapat's hand. "Goodbye, Mr. Shockley."

He smiled and nodded. "The rescue was worth 10,000 points. You are almost over the finish line. Why stop now?"

Seven knew that was a con. Simulations never had a finish line, only a continuous loop, with points stacking up to reach the moon but never quite reaching the stars.

5.3

Where are you?

Friendship Hotel, Sukhumvit Road, Bangkok

Like ice into water and water into steam... Seven continued to fix her gaze at the crate of iceberg water bottles Shockley had left behind. She had never felt more alone and sad. Anger welled up inside as she picked up one of the bottles by the neck and flung it as hard as she could at the sea. It exploded in a star cluster of light, turning the shoreline a silvery glowing white.

As she leaned down for a second bottle of water, she looked to her right. Chinapat was next to her in bed in their Bangkok hotel room. They'd been drinking Mekong whiskey, and the bottles were strewn on the floor. She held an empty bottle in her hand, and as she rolled over she asked Chinapat if he was awake. He'd unhooked a red and blue wire from the insert plates at the base of his skull cables. The first two rows on the consort unit beside the bed flashed a hot white.

"Why does the dolphin simulation always upset you?" he asked. It was like asking an addict why she couldn't go cold turkey.

He gently removed the cables from Seven and let them drop to the side.

She twisted the wires between her thumb and forefinger, and looked up at Chinapat. He was waiting for her answer.

"We're out of the router, right?"

He nodded.

"We're off the grid, right?" she asked.

"Right." That seemed obvious, and he wondered why she asked.

She shook her head. "It's not right. I'm logged at 5.2? And where are you, if you're not at 5.2?"

Chinapat rolled over and grinned into his pillow. She'd confused the "where are you" with the "who are you" matrix.

"Listen," he said, "and they'll tell you themselves." He cranked up the volume on the black console no bigger than a shoebox. Dolphin voices echoed across the room, liming the ceiling with a blanket of white ice crystals. The hotel window overlooking Sukhumvit Road was caked with a half-inch thick sheet of frost. The rising and falling singsong notes, like musical instruments, formed patterns in the ice.

When Shockley opened the door, it was no longer the hotel. They were aboard ship, in the holding tank. As he stepped inside, Shockley handed her a glass filled to the top with pure iceberg water.

"Take another sip and relax. Another ten thousand years will pass in the blink of an eye."

Christopher G. Moore

Canadian Christopher G. Moore is the creator of the award-winning Vincent Calvino crime fiction series and the author of the Land of Smiles Trilogy.

In his former life, he studied at Oxford University and taught law at the University of British Columbia. He wrote radio plays for the CBC and NHK before his first novel was published in New York in 1985, when he promptly left his tenured academic job for an uncertain writing career, leaving his colleagues thinking he was not quite right in the head.

His journey from Canada to Thailand, his adopted home, included some time in Japan in the early 1980s and four years in New York in the late 1980s. In 1988, he came to Thailand to harvest materials to write a book. The visit was meant to be temporary. Two decades and 22 novels later, he is still in Bangkok and far from having exhausted the rich Southeast Asian literary materials. His novels have so far appeared in a dozen languages.

For more information about the author and his books, visit his website: www.cgmoore.com. He also blogs weekly at International Crime Authors: Reality Check: www.internationalcrimeauthors.com.

The Mistress Wants
Her Freedom

Tew Bunnag

Was it destiny? According to Pi Nok there was no
doubt about it. His regular fortune teller in Onnut
market had told him that very morning that it was
going to be a special day, one in which someone
from the past might reappear, and that he should be
prepared. Admittedly he had already put that piece
of cheap, innocuous advice out of his mind by the
time he saw Nong Maew later in the Siam Paragon
shopping centre for their weekly gossip session. Of
course the conversation turned, as always, to her
love life, or rather the lack of it.

"It's so unfair," she was saying as they peered
through the smoky glass display window of a designer
store at the ridiculously expensive pair of red suede
Italian loafers that they both lusted after.

"He'd buy them for his wife, if she asked him.
But I have to wait for him to give me the presents
that he chooses."

Without taking his eyes off the shoes, Pi Nok replied in a sarcastic voice, "You've had a sweet Japanese sports car off him, and a sweet luxury apartment and a wardrobe full of clothes and your regular little envelope…"

"All right, he takes good care of me," said Nong Maew, giggling. "But why do I have to wait around for him all the time? I'm fed up with it. I'm twenty-three. I want a life!"

This was a line he had heard a dozen times—the unhappiness of the kept woman—and he never found it convincing. Usually, out of friendship, he commiserated with her, but today her words grated on him. Having lost his own foreign benefactor the previous year and now working in a massage parlour, struggling to keep afloat, he found it hard to sympathize with her poor little mistress number.

"Well, you can always go back to your old life," he said cattily.

Nong Maew was annoyed at this remark. Even though Pi Nok was her closest friend and confidant, her "gig", he had no right to be unkind. She did not ever want to be reminded of what she had done or what she had been. Without answering him, and with a petulant swish of her young, lithe body, sheathed in its blue polka dot dress, she turned and headed straight for the escalator.

Pi Nok walked behind her and said, teasingly: "Don't be so touchy. You know you're beyond all that now."

"Oh, you're such a bitch today. I don't believe it!" she half-whispered, and they both laughed out loud.

As she looked up towards the floor above, she stopped in her tracks and, to Pi Nok's surprise, took hold of his hand and squeezed it tightly. Without turning around, she said in panic: "That's him with his wife. And that must be his grandson. Don't look, they're coming down. Oh no! What do I do? Where do I go?"

Without hesitating, Pi Nok pulled her gently onto the escalator. Now he too looked up and saw a man with grey hair carrying a yellow plastic shopping bag. He was in a dark, well-cut suit and looked like a businessman taking time off from the office to do some shopping with the family. Next to him was a stout woman in a Thai silk outfit, wearing thick sunglasses and a complicated, stiff hairdo, and behind them a small boy whose hand was touching the man's shoulder. As they came closer, to his utter astonishment Pi Nok recognized the man's face. "It's destiny," he thought to himself, suddenly remembering the fortune teller's prediction.

Nong Maew had never divulged her patron's real name. She always referred to him as Darling, using the English word but stressing the last syllable so that it sounded Thai. It was the way they addressed each other, she had said when she first told Pi Nok about the man who had picked her up in the club two years earlier and who then, one day, out of the blue, proposed that she should be his mistress. She had added that he was good-looking and fit for his sixty-eight years, and that, naturally, he was loaded. This last detail was the most important one. For why else would she be wasting her youth on a married man nearly four times her age who had no intention of committing himself to her in a million years?

As the family passed Nong Maew and Pi Nok on their way down to the second floor, the man she referred to as Darling looked over in their direction. The woman was turning the other way while the boy's attention was drawn to a colourful film poster that was hanging off the balcony. Nong Maew did not return the gaze. Instead she put on a hard, artificial expression of indifference and fixed her attention on the space in front of her. In doing so, she was unaware that it was not at her that Darling was directing his gaze, but at her companion, for as they passed each other with only the two feet between them, he too recognized Pi Nok and in that moment, involuntarily, his whole face lit up with a spontaneous expression that can only be described as remembered pleasure.

They were in a Japanese restaurant on the ground floor. Pi Nok swallowed his mouthful of sushi and said nothing for a while. His fine features registered a moment of choked sadness, enhanced by the pungency of the wasabi dip. He had been explaining to Nong Maew, who sat in attentive silence, how he had met her "Darling" Khun Taworn two years before she did, what had gone on between them and how they had parted company.

"He went to China, on business, and the club was closed down overnight while he was away. That's why we lost touch, and after that I never saw him again," he said, continuing his tale and addressing these words to his own reflection in the window as if reminiscing a private and painful episode.

If Nong Maew was surprised by what she was hearing, she managed not to show it. She had long suspected Darling of being bi, but she had not expected her intuition to be confirmed by such a personal connection. With her best friend, of all people! And now Pi Nok was trying to paint what must have been a professional encounter into some kind of grand love affair. She kept her composure on the outside, but her mind was swirling, especially when he had the nerve to try convincing her to share Darling with him.

"Come on, he's got enough for both of us," he pleaded unashamedly.

Nong Maew, who had hardly touched her food, took this as the cue to comment on what Pi Nok had been saying. She chose her words with care and put on a fine show of well-tempered indignation. In a high-minded tone she told Pi Nok that the supposed romance between him and Khun Taworn had taken place in a gay brothel, albeit a high-class one, but a brothel nevertheless. And how dare he try to muscle in on her good fortune when she had done all the running? But even as she was discouraging him from making a play on her Darling, Nong Maew was well aware that Pi Nok, given his hunger and lascivious nature, was probably already planning his moves.

Khun Taworn, one of the wealthiest industrialists in Thailand, was a prime catch for any ambitious hustler. Nong Maew herself could not believe her luck when, true to his word, he installed her in the condo by the river, because she had not made any effort at all to lure him exclusively to herself. He had picked her in the "Twilight", an exclusive private club where she was one of the part-timers who worked there for extra cash. You had to be both beautiful and discreet because the clientele consisted of the very rich and powerful of the land. Khun Taworn had chosen her out of a roomful of young women who looked like starlets, and in their first sexual encounter in the VIP suite he seemed pleased with her services. After three visits he asked her out to dinner, which was quite normal and encouraged by the management since it reinforced the illusion that the girls were not professionals but companions who were sufficiently attracted to accept the invitation.

That night, in a candlelit French restaurant, Khun Taworn had explained that he was thinking of returning to politics, reminding her that ten years earlier, when she was only a young girl, he had been tipped to win the election to be leader of his party. But he had been betrayed, he was quick to add. Now he was ready to return to the fray. Because of this he could no longer risk being seen anywhere that could cause a scandal for him or his family. He had decided not to go to places like the "Twilight" anymore. But he wanted to continue seeing her. And that was when he asked her outright to become his mistress. Without letting her have time to think about his proposition—as though, in the style of men used to having their way, he was sure that she would not resist—he went on to give her the details of the arrangement that he had worked out and which, in fact, were so generous that she would have been foolish to have refused.

Nong Maew had been overwhelmed by his offer. It meant the end of having to make all the effort of going to work and worrying about paying off the debts that she had accumulated and living in shared, cramped accommodation. It would give her time to go back to finish her university degree, if she chose to do so. And if she played her cards well, she could even set up her own business one day. Suddenly the future was wide open. Everything was possible, and all she had to do was to give pleasure to a man whose vanity, with the help of Viagra, was soothed by possessing her firm, trim body. So, without thinking of the consequences, she accepted.

At first she had been drunk with her new life. Moving out of the small rented apartment she shared with two other working girls into a pad in an exclusive condo with its own small swimming pool on the balcony and a view of the city spreading out in all directions was like arriving in the Deva realm of the angels. Khun Taworn visited her three or four times a week, often bringing a bottle of champagne and a little gift. They never went out again after that evening in the French restaurant, but delicious, elaborate meals were ordered in from the best establishments in Bangkok. In those early days, when he had finished talking about himself, he would ask her about how she was spending her spare time and whether she was happy. But as the months rolled slowly by, he became less and less interested in what she did or thought or felt. He would arrive and take his pill and wait for the effect to kick in and then fuck her as though he was offloading some pent-up aggression. Then, afterwards, while she massaged his back, he would ramble on about politics or his family life. Often he would tell her how difficult his relationship with his wife was. It seemed that she hated him. Once Nong Maew made the mistake of giving him her opinion about his dysfunctional marriage, but the way that he cut her short made her realize that he required neither her response nor her sympathy. He merely needed her to be there as a beautiful trinket to bolster his self-esteem and as a receptacle into which he could pour his artificially stimulated desire.

Now, two years later, she was desperate with the sheer boredom of her existence. Darling's visits were less frequent, and when he dropped by, she found it harder and harder to play the role of dumb listener. In short, she had discovered that the routine of being somebody's mistress just did not suit her character. Being a sex object made her feel like an idiot. Her cocooned comfort did not compensate for the sense of despair that overcame her with growing frequency. There were days when she wanted to pack up and leave. But then she could never forget the money and all the perks that came with her status. She had become used to the ease and luxury, and she knew all too well that to regain her freedom, she had to be prepared to give up this honey-coated lifestyle that everyone she knew and probably most of the country dreamed of tasting. For them it would always remain a distant dream. But for her it was what she awoke to every morning. This was what made it a tough choice.

While he was waxing lyrical about his affair with Darling, Pi Nok had spared no details, as if to prove that he, as a man, could do a better job at satisfying Khun Taworn's desires than she, as a woman, could ever imagine. While she listened to his lurid descriptions of her Darling's likes and dislikes, Nong Maew's mind was busy weighing up her options. And later, when she was trying to dissuade her friend from competing with her for Darling's favours, and even going so far as to say that, if he decided to do so, it was going to mean the end of their friendship, she knew that her efforts at dissuasion would only challenge him to go ahead and run after her man as soon as the opportunity arose.

A voice in the back of her mind was telling her how easy it was to merely say to Pi Nok: "Okay, have him. He's yours if you think you can really catch him." And she would be free. It was what she wanted, after all. But another voice, the promptings of Lobha, or Greed, was already suggesting ways of making use of the information that Pi Nok was giving her to achieve the same goal without losing the benefits that she had come to feel she deserved.

That same evening Darling visited her. They greeted each other warmly. Neither mentioned the encounter on the escalator at the shopping mall. He declared immediately that he was not in the mood for sex. He told her to open the champagne and then, after taking a big gulp from the glass that she handed him, said casually: "And who was that boy you were with this morning?"

Nong Maew had expected the question.

"Oh, that was an old friend of mine from university," she answered brightly.

"Are you going out together?"

Nong Maew smiled broadly before replying: "No, he's gay. Couldn't you tell, darling?"

Khun Taworn nodded his head without changing his expression and took another big sip of his champagne. Nong Maew felt that it was the moment to take the gamble.

"Would you like to meet him, darling? He's very interesting. He used to study economics, you know. He's brilliant. He told me that he recognized you straightaway because he is an admirer of your party. He thinks you'll win the next election for sure, especially with that line you're pushing about the family and the community."

Darling took a couple of seconds to scrutinize Nong Maew's face for any sign that she was being anything less than ingenuous. Satisfied, he nodded again.

"Why not? Yes, I'll meet your friend. If he's as clever as you say, I might be able to use him in my research team."

Nong Maew smiled inwardly. This was her first step to freedom.

During the days that followed Nong Maew was in a strange mood. The fact that her plan involved betraying both her friend and her benefactor was something that filled her with conflicting emotions. It was not exactly that she felt guilty for what she was doing, but there was, nevertheless, a certain unpleasantness that she could not easily shake off. After all, Pi Nok had never done her any harm. On the contrary, he had always been patient, supportive and generous to her when she was down. As for her Darling, he had given her a few years of affluence that she had not expected to come her way. The only real complaint against him was that he had treated her as a body and nothing else, but then all the men she had met, with the exception of Pi Nok, had done that.

To counter her uncomfortably acute sense of disloyalty to both of them, Nong Maew kept reminding herself what her mother had taught her when she was a little girl: that you are totally on your own in this world, and you have to look after your own interests first. And in the end her mind yielded up the justifications she needed to go ahead with her treacherous scheme. After that it was merely a matter of finding the nerve to carry it through.

With her newly found sense of purpose, Nong Maew now took the decisive step towards her freedom. She called Pi Nok and asked him casually if he had any luck contacting Khun Taworn. Pi Nok, thinking that Nong Maew was provoking him, answered coldly: "I'm in no rush. I'm not that desperate, whatever you may think. I'll get to him when I want."

"Well, then, you can come to dinner," she said. "He's interested in seeing you."

There was silence on the other end. She could sense Pi Nok's excitement. She knew him.

"What's your game?" he finally asked.

"I've been thinking, that's all. I don't want us to be rivals. And I know you'll find some way of meeting him. When you're determined, there's no stopping you. So why can't we be cool about it?"

Pi Nok, touched and flattered by her words even reassured her that he would never try to steal Darling away from her.

Satisfied that there had as yet been no communication between Pi Nok and Darling, Nong Maew sent Khun Taworn a text on his mobile phone. It was a rule that she never called him directly because, given his position, he was afraid that his phone was bugged. His paranoia had affected her to such an extent that she often imagined someone listening in to her own phone and was constantly noting little odd sounds which she could not account for. But that day, as part of her plan to go against the guidelines, she decided to take the risk and sent him a blatantly lascivious text message telling him how she was sad and lonely and needed to see him urgently. She made it sound like she was a bitch in heat. He was around that very afternoon and made no mention of her transgression. Having taken the medicine in the limousine, as soon as he was through the door he was ripping off his jacket and was soon on top of her. Passion over, he said that he had a meeting to attend and could not stay. He showered quickly and began to put his clothes back on.

"I am angry with you," she blurted out, as she lay exhausted and naked on the bed while she watched him dressing.

"You and my friend were lovers once, weren't you? He told me, so don't deny it. He gave me all the sordid details." Her voice was more hurt than angry.

Khun Taworn stopped what he was doing, looked at her for a while in surprise and then burst out laughing.

"So he told you."

"And you're still hot for him. I know you are."

He made no reply to this last remark, which she had spat out accusingly.

"I want out! I can't stand it. It's awful."

She was now raising her voice to match her emotions.

"Come on, calm down. Don't be jealous." Khun Taworn's face suddenly looked weary and dark.

"No! I mean it," Nong Maew continued, undeterred. "I've had enough. You don't really care for me, and now I know that you prefer men. It's obvious. So let me go. I'll fix you up with him. He can take over this apartment if you like. Just give me something for the years you've had from me, and I'll be out of your life."

Nong Maew was sobbing now, and as she did so, she remembered Darling's hard advice to her at their first dinner in the French restaurant, when he was setting out the terms of their contract: "I don't want any emotions in this. If you're going to get possessive and jealous and cry because I don't love you and that kind of stuff, then don't even think of being with me because I don't have time for any of it." He had said it all bluntly enough.

Now, even without looking up at him, she could feel his annoyance and realized that she had reached his point of intolerance. So with every second her sobs become more intense. She was burying her head in the pillow and gripping it with both her hands.

"Oh, stop it! That's enough!" Khun Taworn was shouting as he closed his ears with his palms. "I told you that I can't stand this kind of thing. And by the way, I told you never to get in touch with me by phone unless it's an absolute emergency. You're getting to be a real pain in the neck."

"Then let me go! I'll leave you in peace. I'll let you have Pi Nok, even if it breaks me up. But I can't share you with him or anyone else anymore. It killed me to see you with your wife the other day. I can't live with jealousy. I just can't. I'll do something to myself that you'll regret if you carry on treating me like this."

Eventually she calmed down, but not before Khun Taworn agreed to let her have her freedom along with an interesting sum that would last her for a couple of years—a pittance for him, but a golden handshake for her. In gratitude she told him that she would arrange a farewell dinner, so that he could be properly reintroduced to her friend Pi Nok. It would serve as a kind of handing over ceremony. Khun Taworn, relieved that he was getting a hysterical, jealous girl off his hands and at the same time overjoyed that he was rediscovering a treasure he thought he had lost for good, accepted Nong Maew's offer without hesitation. So a date was fixed.

If Nong Maew had been content with what she had achieved so far with her convincing theatrics, she might have had the freedom she desired the next day when Khun Taworn made the transfer to her account of the sum he had promised. But things had gone so well up till then that she was encouraged to carry her plan through to the final stage. In fact, by now she could not stop the momentum of her actions. For the first time in years she felt alive and creative. But apart from the existential high that she was enjoying, it came down to the fact that she wanted much more than she had been offered, and she was sure it was within her reach. This was why she had suggested the dinner.

The scenario that she had rehearsed in her mind over and over again required one outsider. This was an electrician she had befriended while working at the "Twilight." He had already done some work for her when she had first moved in. She called him now and offered him a decent fee to set up a hidden camera system in the apartment. This was something that presented no problem whatsoever to him, and he managed to get it done in a couple of days. Nong Maew's plan with the cameras was that on the night of the dinner she would find an excuse to leave the two men alone at some point. They would not think it strange, given the fact that she was playing the pimp for them. There was a special switch near the front door which would activate the cameras as she left. If everything that Pi Nok had told her was true, then they would be all over each other even before she had reached the ground floor in the lift. She planned to be away long enough for Khun Taworn to leave, with or without Pi Nok. He never stayed later than 9:30. If they were still there, Nong Maew was quite prepared for a threesome. She had covered all the possible scenarios. The only gamble, which seemed to her a sure bet, was that the two men would hit it off.

The tapes that she was going to obtain from that evening of gay pleasure between a prominent member of Thai society and a handsome young hustler would set her up for life. She would not be too greedy. Like those Hollywood divorcees she had read about, Nong Maew would merely ask for, and receive, a monthly income from Khun Taworn that would keep her in her accustomed lifestyle in a different part of the city, or in another city in Asia—

Hong Kong, perhaps, or Singapore—in a bigger and more luxurious apartment. In return she would agree not to sell the tapes to the other political parties or put them up on YouTube. And just in case he had any ideas of arranging for her disappearance from the face of the earth, she was taking out insurance, so that if anything happened to her, the tapes would be immediately made public.

It seemed foolproof.

On the night in question everything went even more smoothly than she had envisaged. The food came from an Italian restaurant and was beautifully presented. The wine, Brunello di Montalcino, cost $200 a bottle. Khun Taworn had asked for it especially. It was his party, and he wanted the best. Over dinner she noticed that Pi Nok was already tickling Darling's leg with his toe under the table—a good sign for things to come. As for Khun Taworn, he was aglow with lust, and the Brunello di Montalcino made him more verbose than usual. When she brought the dessert into the room, Nong Maew suddenly gave out a convincing cry of regret.

"Oh, I am so sorry. I forgot the Patron tequila in the lobby of the Oriental. I was having tea there this afternoon, and I must have left it on a table."

Patron tequila was Khun Taworn's favourite drink.

"And this is such a special occasion, this lovely reunion. Look, if you two gentlemen will excuse me, I'll just nip down there. I won't be more than twenty minutes. It's just up the road. Of course I could call them and ask for the concierge to send it… but I'm sure you'll have a lot of catching up to do while I'm out…"

Neither Khun Taworn nor Pi Nok objected to her suggestion. By now they seemed so besotted with each other that they were only too pleased for her to leave them alone. So, making sure that she flicked on the switch as she left the apartment, Nong Maew left the two of them to what she knew was going to be a torrid renewal of friendship.

Precisely an hour later Nong Maew returned to the apartment, having collected the bottle of tequila, not from the Oriental Hotel, but from a nearby bar in Sathorn Road where she often went. There she had ordered a dry martini in anticipatory celebration and flicked through a fashion magazine, all the while allowing herself to daydream of the clothes she would buy, of the places in the world that she would visit, of the freedom that she would finally have.

When she returned to the condo she was mildly surprised to find that the men were still in the bedroom. She could hear the sound of their lovemaking as she walked through the front door, and it was so abandoned that it made her blush for a moment. And yet a second later she registered that there was something wrong. Her eyes scanned the living room. Clothes were strewn everywhere. She looked over to the bedroom and saw that the door was slightly ajar and a light flickered from inside. The sound of sexual pleasure was now pulsating. Instinctively she hesitated before taking another step forward. Just then a fit-looking young man with close-cropped hair, dressed in a pink polo shirt and chinos stepped out of the room in such a nonchalant way, as though he lived there in the apartment, that Nong Maew suddenly felt she was in a dream, dislocated somewhere between the familiar and the unexpected. Then, as she began to open her mouth to speak, she saw a gun in his hand that was pointed directly at her heart, and her whole being went cold. The man nodded slowly as though he understood how terrified she was.

"I'm sorry, sister," he said, as the sounds of love from the bedroom subsided. "It's just a job."

Khun Taworn's wife sat on the edge of the bed, wearing a cream silk dressing gown. Her wig was off, and she was rubbing moisturizer slowly over her pale, bald cranium. When she finished, she wiped her hands on a small towel, leaned over to the bedside table and poured herself a glass of tequila. When the mobile phone shuddered to life, she did not rush to answer it but stretched her free hand behind her to pat the body that was stirring—the beautiful, naked body of the young actress she was grooming to be a star.

"I have to answer this, darling." She too used the English word but pronounced it correctly. "Go back to sleep."

Now she picked up the phone and took a sip from her glass.

"It's done," said the man's voice on the other end.

"No hitches?"

"None. But the girl was making a home movie. That's why she called the electrician from the "Twilight" the other day."

"Then he has to go too. And get rid of the tapes."

"No problem."

"Tell me. How was it? My husband?"

"He promised me the moon."

"He was always a bad liar."

"The gay boy cried. The girl tried to talk her way out of it. She wasn't making sense. She kept on saying that all she wanted was her freedom."

"She should have taken the money and run. Why are people so greedy? Anyway, now she's free."

"The papers will have a field day."

"Yes, it'll be juicy. You've done well. Thank you."

With her drink in her hand she walked to the window with its view of the city stretching south. Her sad eyes looked down at the lights twinkling in the streets below and at the giant billboards on the

Hansum Man

Timothy Hallinan

The room was dark when he opened his eyes. For a moment he was confused; the window was in the wrong place. Had he been sleeping with his head at the foot of the bed? His sleep was thin these days, thinner than the worn sheet that covered him, but he didn't usually move around that much. Or did he?

Oh. The new apartment. The one he still couldn't navigate in the dark without bumping into something. Unlike the shopfront he had lived above for all those years, the two rooms with the wood-shuttered windows that you could prop open with a length of doweling. Cool cement floors.

He sat up with a soft grunt and put his feet down. Carpet. Window on the right. Not the shophouse then, the apartment. What had happened to the shophouse?

Now that he knew which room he was in, his hand could find the surprisingly heavy little brass lamp on the bed table. It put out just enough light to show him a heavily shadowed room, almost too small for the bed and the table, with a wide recessed closet yawning open in one corner, one of its sliding doors derailed and leaning at a seasick angle against the wall. His clothes, what remained of them, were hanging any old way, like a mixed crowd of birds pecking seed on a pavement before they lift off and sort themselves into flocks. The air conditioner sat aslant in the window and silent, since he had decided long ago to live with the heat. After all, he'd *chosen* the heat. The bathroom, over there, through that grimy door. He reminded himself again to take a sponge to the door.

With his sight restored, the world tilted slightly and snapped into place with an almost audible click. The shophouse had been demolished long ago, along with the whole neighborhood, a cluster of two- and three-story structures of inky, mildewed concrete, spiderwebbed with black electrical wires, built on either side of a *soi* almost too narrow for cars—paved over one of Bangkok's lost canals. A neighborhood where people knew each other, talked to each other when they met, laughed good-naturedly at his occasional sallies into Thai. All the buildings gone now, knocked into dust and chunks of cement.

How *noisy* it had been, the machines growling like big dogs at the buildings before taking bites out of them, some of the people staring dolefully from across the *soi*, looking like attendees at a cremation.

He got up and launched himself toward the bathroom, feeling a light fizziness in his head. Had he drunk before going to bed? Stupid question. And what time was it, anyway? It had been weeks since he'd been able to find the heavy steel Rolex his father had given him to take to Nam. He'd promised his parents he'd keep it on California time so he'd be with them whenever he looked at it, but that hadn't lasted. And neither, after all these years, had the Rolex. He'd bought a counterfeit at a sidewalk market, and as he turned on the bathroom light, the watch gleamed at him and informed him it was 10:21. So he'd slept through the day's heat, and outside, the Bangkok he loved best had blinked into life.

The bathroom mirror showed him the grandfather or great-grandfather of Wallace, never Wally, Palmer, shockingly old. His head of dark, curly hair had been replaced by a few long, iron-gray strands, inexplicably straight, that pasted themselves across his spotted scalp. He'd played a few times with the strands, trying to comb them lower on his forehead to simulate a real hairline, but the last time he'd done it the phrase "turban renewal" had flashed through his mind, and he'd laughed and abandoned the effort. At least his hair didn't stand up on end and lasso the light, the silver-beech forest of frizziness that haloed the heads of so many old guys.

Old guys.

Wallace said, "Shit," avoiding looking at the devastation that was his neck, and picked up his toothbrush.

Someone knocked on the door in the living room.

"It's always something," Wallace said, although he was aware that, lately, it hadn't been. He leaned heavily against the sink and waited, hoping whoever it was would go away, but a moment later he heard three knocks, louder this time, and—muffled by the door—a *basso profundo* voice called, "Vallace? You are in zere, Vallace?"

Leon, Wallace thought with a surge of despair. Leon Hofstedler, the most boring man in Bangkok. So boring, Leon's friend Ernie had once said, that you'd avoid him if he was the first person you'd seen in a month. What had happened to Ernie? Ernie always made him laugh.

The knocks sounded again, loud as kicks. "Vallace? I need to hear you talking. Everybody in ze bar asks, is Vallace okay?"

Leon wasn't going away. Leon had nothing better to do with his life than to stand in that hallway, kicking Wallace's crappy door and singing German opera for everybody in the building to hear. One of Wallace's life principles floated up toward him like a message in that magic eight-ball everyone used to have, *Always move toward trouble, not away from it.* In the jungle, don't turn your back. On the city street, don't turn your back.

Don't turn your back on Leon Hofstedler.

The idea of Leon being dangerous made Wallace laugh as he went back into the bedroom, heading toward the living room. Wallace had lived with *dangerous* day and night for three tours of sweating, steaming, leech-ridden, blood-stinking duty. The only thing Leon had ever killed was time. Wallace thought he'd like to say that to Ernie. Ernie always looked surprised before he laughed, as though it startled him that other people were funny.

"Coming, Ernie," Wallace called. He remembered to look down at himself and was reassured to see that he'd gone to sleep fully dressed.

"Ernie?" Hofstedler bellowed though the door. "Zis is not Ernie. Ernie—*mein Gott!*—Ernie is a zousand years ago. You should not be alone so much."

"I'm not alone," Wallace said, undoing the door's assortment of locks—a joke, given that the door itself was made of soda cracker. "I've got three Balinese girl scouts with me." He opened the door on the mountain that was Leon Hofstedler.

Hofstedler, his magisterial bulk draped in one of the many-pocketed safari shirts he had made for him a dozen at a time by a Thai seamstress, narrowed his eyes as if trying to see through Wallace to the wall behind him. He said, "Ernie?"

"Been thinking about him," Wallace said.

179

Hofstedler continued to study Wallace's face. After a moment he gave a grudging grunt. "I tell zem you look okay."

"Of course I'm okay," Wallace said around the bloom of irritation in his chest. "Why wouldn't I be okay?"

Hofstedler shrugged. "Zey worry. You not coming, night after night. You know, thinking maybe…" Whatever they were thinking, it was too dire for Hofstedler to voice it.

"Just a little busy," Wallace said, putting some weight on the door. "You tell them I'm fine and say hello for me, 'kay?" He pushed the door closed on Hofstedler, completing the sentence in his mind, … *whoever they are.*

A shower. That was what he needed, a shower and some clean clothes. *Jah*, it was Jah he wanted to see. Whip thin, tousle-haired Jah, who went with him to Don Muang Airport the first time he flew back home and cried inconsolably at the departure gate. And was there, jumping up and down like a teenager, when he came back. Running at him from thirty yards away and leaping on him, her legs twined around his waist, as all the other passengers stared.

He thought, *Don Muang? Do international flights still go through Don Muang?* It sounded wrong, but he shrugged it off, along with his shirt and trousers, and padded toward the shower. *The girls may be professionals,* he thought, *but they're still Thai. It shows respect when you come to them clean.*

The road was far too wide.

He came out of the narrow corridor that led from the apartment house's single clanking elevator, extravagantly scented with cat piss, feeling light on his feet, decisive and clear-headed, as though he were back walking point in Nam. But as the door closed behind him, he saw the road and took a stumble that forced him to step forward or fall on his face. It was six lanes wide, the road, a Mekong River of lights, the demon-red of tail-lights, the hard diamond-yellow of headlights. He stood there for a second, loose-jointed and irresolute, as the narrow *soi* in front of the old shophouse thinned, shimmered and disappeared, giving way to the street he'd moved to.

He said, "Sukhumvit," identifying it, and the kernel of unease in his chest softened at the name. His own voice reassured him. "Sukhumvit." Where was he going? Yes, Jah. Jah worked at... Thai... Thai something. Thai Paradise?

Well, he knew where it was, even if the name eluded him. He stepped to the curb, one arm upraised, palm down, a gesture of long habit. A couple of taxis slowed, but he waved them by until he could flag a tuk-tuk, which almost ran over Wallace's foot. The driver was a skinny, dark kid with a shadowy mustache and a long fall of black hair dipping over one eye. Wallace climbed in, sat back and said, "Golden Mile."

The tuk-tuk vibrated as its little two-stroke engine chugged and popped, but it didn't move. The boy's eyes found Wallace's in the mirror. "You say where?"

"Golden Mile, the Golden Mile," Wallace said. He smiled so his impatience wouldn't show but got no smile in return.

"Hotel?" the boy asked.

"No, no, no. Golden Mile. Bars. New Petchburi Road."

"Okay," the boy said with a nod. "Golden Mile. Petchburi."

"Thai *Heaven*," Wallace said as the cab pulled out. Jah worked at Thai Heaven.

"Okay, boss," the boy said, his eyes on the traffic behind. "Golden Mile."

He sat back and closed his eyes. The exhaust was perfume, the chuk-chuk of the engine, music. Oh, how he had fallen in love with Bangkok on his first R&R, after six months of duty, his feet rotting with the damp, whole colonies of exotic parasites claiming his intestines, his soul knotted with death. The girls in the villages they defended, sometimes by burning them, looked at Wallace and the others in his platoon with terror and revulsion, which the Americans occasionally earned. Three times, men he knew well had turned bestial on the floor of some thatched shack, impatiently taking turns on a girl barely out of childhood. Leaving behind, suddenly tiny on the floor, the crushed and sobbing remnant of a human being, and once even less than that.

And then, after a copter out and a few hours in a plane, he was here, in the city of joy. Smiles everywhere, food everywhere, everything cheap and easy, and girls who *loved* him. Girls like nutmeg, girls like cinnamon, girls who blended into a single smile, a single "no problem" as he took them, in threes and fours at first, like a starving man sweeping a whole table full of food to himself, and then, as faces and names emerged, one by one. Jah, Noi, Lek, Tuum. Sometimes staying with one of them for days on end. Falling asleep beside her on clean sheets in a cool room. Warm breath on his chest. Safe.

Hansum man, Jah called him. *Teerak*, Jah called him, Thai for sweetheart. Wallet, Jah called him, and he thought it was her joke until he realized that Thais couldn't pronounce a sibilant at the end of a word, and she thought she was saying his name, the same way she said "Santa Claut." He took to calling himself Wallet, appreciating the name's appropriateness even if Jah didn't understand it. He was lean and young and handsome, and the way Jah eyed the other girls when they were together made him think of someone driving into the old neighborhood at the wheel of a sports car.

The first night that she stayed with him, just as he'd been about to drop off, she'd raised herself onto one elbow, the bedside lamp creating a circle of reflected light on the smooth skin of her shoulder, and said: "This room. How much?"

He'd told her. Her eyes had gone round and her mouth had dropped open, and she'd emitted a sound like a puff of steam, and then she was up and pulling on her clothes, her shoulders high and rigid with determination. A moment later, the door closed behind her.

He thought, *I didn't pay her.* For a moment he panicked, thinking she might have taken the money from his pocket, but it was right there. He was refolding his pants when the phone rang and the desk clerk said, "Mr. Palmer? The young lady has renegotiated your room rate. You've been given a discount of thirty percent." And then she'd knocked on the door, and she had whipped her T-shirt over her head and was hitting him on the back with it before he closed the door behind her.

She'd cried at the airport.

She's going to be so happy, he thought. *I'll walk into Thai Heaven and she'll scream, "Hansum man!" and abandon whoever she was sitting with and run across the club to him. With that smile, brighter than Liberty's torch...*

"Okay," the driver said. "Golden Mile."

The tuk-tuk stopped. Wallace had his hand in his pocket when the boy said, "One hundred twenty baht."

"*One hundred twenty?*" Wallace sat there, a wad of money in his hand. "*Twenty*, twenty baht."

"One-twenty," the boy said. "Twenty baht, one hundred year ago, maybe."

"Forty," Wallace snapped. "That's it." He dropped two twenties over the back of the seat, feeling the rudeness of the gesture, and climbed down onto the pavement, tuning out the boy's yells. A narrow street, nowhere near as wide as New Petchburi. A couple of cars, each with a wheel up on the sidewalk, were almost too close together to allow him to pass, but he turned sideways to squeeze through and heard the tuk-tuk putter away, the boy still shouting angrily.

Once up on the sidewalk, he stopped, looking up.

It *was* a hotel. He was in front of a hotel. Huge letters on the side of the building said "ROYAL SUITES." Up and down the street were business buildings, some new, some old. Nothing he recognized.

A uniformed doorman came through the revolving door, eyebrows lifted in a question, and Wallace crossed the gritty red carpet laid down in front of the door. The man glanced at him and said, "Sir?" No more than mild politeness.

Wallace said, "The Golden Mile?"

The doorman lifted a hand, palm up, and brought it shoulder high to indicate the hotel behind him. "Hotel," he said. "Hotel is owned by Golden Mile."

Wallace was already shaking his head. "No, no. No, not a hotel. *The Golden Mile*. Bars, restaurants..." He ran out of words. "*Bars*."

Backing toward the door, the doorman said, "Sorry, sorry. Don't know. Maybe..." He pointed across the street and to his left, in the general direction of New Petchburi Road, gleaming a long, dark block away. The street the hotel was on was a *soi*, relatively narrow, with the hotel sprouting from a row of shorter, darker structures, and here and there a shrubbed chain-link fence. "Over there, maybe. Other side."

"No," Wallace said, but he was already turning, already forgetting the doorman. "It's this side. I'm sure it's this side."

Although there was no oncoming traffic, he crossed the *soi* at an angle, as though carried by the same current that would bear the cars along. Once across, he lowered his head and struck out at a brisk walk with the lights of New Petchburi behind him, half-certain that in a hundred yards or so, there would be light and noise and the sound of English.

But there wasn't. Thinking about Jah, he passed a narrow cross-street, almost turning into it, but it was too dark. *Bars are lighted. The tuk-tuk driver brought me to the wrong place and tried to cheat me. Bangkok is changing.* He walked more briskly, leaving New Petchburi farther behind, moving in the certainty that sheer decisiveness would get him where he wanted to go.

It wasn't hard for him to imagine, in front of him, the strings of Christmas lights and the scattering of neon, the neon not as plentiful or as vulgar as at Patpong, that upstart street, but enough to lure him forward, enough to suggest the warmth and friendliness of a bar, the smell of the beer, the music of women's voices. The softness of women's faces. Jah's face, the slightly overlong upper lip, the permanent upward curl at the corners of her mouth that made her look like she was always suppressing a laugh. He could almost smell her, the salt sea-smell of her secret places.

Another cross-street approached, promising in its furtiveness, but he stopped, the street slipping from his mind as he registered the floating ribbon of concrete suspended against the dark sky far, far in front of him: an elevated highway. *That's why I'm turned around,* he thought. *That wasn't there before,* and the moment he had articulated the thought, he saw the boys.

Three of them, maybe eighteen or nineteen years old, facing inward in a tight circle around a faint glow of light, as though they were warming themselves at a candle. Wallace felt his chest, which had begun to feel cramped, expand, felt his lungs fill with air as certainty coursed through him. Boys always knew where the action was. And he liked Thai teenagers, so open and friendly, unlike the sour, angry, over-privileged American kids with their long, dirty hair and thrift-store clothes, the ones who had sneered at him, shouted at him, when he went home. The pretty girl, her hair wild curls down her slender back, who spat at him. He felt a smile stake claim to his face.

As he approached, he called out, *"Sawatdee."*

And time went wrong. The comfort and assurance and youth drained out of him as the boys turned and separated, and he saw their faces, despite his efforts to keep them young and friendly, turn old. He saw, in one blunt-force glance, the glittering eyes, the crumpled tinfoil pipe, the disposable lighter with something jammed into the jet to create a thin blue needle of flame. Smelled the sweet metham-phetamine smoke curling from the sizzling pills at the bottom of the pipe.

"Hey, Papa," one of them said. Smoke snaked out of his mouth and he squinted against it.

"Never mind," Wallace said, shaking his head. "No problem." He angled across the sidewalk to the road, intending to cross. The block was dark and quite deserted, no cars in sight. Nowhere to go.

"Pa*pa!*" the man called, following. Maybe 23, 24, gaunt and dirty, with lank, greasy hair and a smile that looked stolen pasted to his face. "Papa, got money for friends? Got baht, got dollar?"

"No." Wallace saw the other two men floating along behind the leader, one of them with the foil pipe at his lips, a red glow lighting the upper half of a misshapen face, crimped on one side as though someone had pressed it in with the heel of a hand before the bones hardened. "Go away."

"Nowhere here to go," the leader said, picking up his pace and angling across the *soi* toward Wallace. "Give money, we take taxi, go. Okay, Papa?" He spread his hands to show they were empty. "Then no problem, yes?"

Wallace felt a flare of young man's anger. He said, "Fuck off. Get your own money and leave me alone."

"Ooooooohhhhh, Papa," the boy said. He called something in Thai, and the other two laughed. The one with the crimped head stuck out his chest and beat it, gorilla-style, and they all laughed again. The two who were farther away were closing in, and within a few seconds all three of them would be within striking distance.

Always move toward trouble, Wallace thought, and he drifted toward the closest boy, saying, "What is it? What is it you want?" He cupped his ear and leaned toward the boy whose grin hardened as he came up directly beside Wallace...

...who put every ounce of strength he possessed into a much-practiced but very rusty side-kick that nevertheless hit the boy square on the outside of the knee, and as he went down, yelling in pain and shock, Wallace knew the cartilage was damaged, and by the time the boy hit the pavement with all his weight on the other knee and shouted at the new pain, Wallace was running.

The *soi* juddered by as he strained, hoisting leaden legs—only thirty or forty feet along and already winded for Christ's sake, but hearing no feet behind him. He dared a glance over his shoulder and saw the two other boys lifting the leader to his feet, the leader screaming after him, pointing an outstretched hand like a rifle, hopping on one leg. The other leg, the one Wallace had damaged, was lifted and bent like a stork's. Wallace faced forward again and found a burst of speed from somewhere, although he knew in the part of his mind that was keeping score that two of them could catch up to him in a minute or less if they abandoned the injured boy and ran full out.

He came to a cross-street and slowed. From somewhere in the past, the information assembled itself: he was running on Soi Jarurat, maybe Petchburi 13. To his left, the cross-street went only a short way and hooked left again, back toward the big road. To the right, he had no idea.

Thai Heaven had been nowhere near here.

If he went left and then left again, trying to get back to the bright lights of New Petchburi Road, the boys might divide up, one staying behind him and the other two running back to the last cross-street to meet him head-on—what he learned in the jungle to call a pincer movement. If I go right, he thought, they can't cut me off.

He was laboring now. His lungs felt like he'd inhaled fire, and the pulse at his throat was as forceful as a tapping thumb. There had to be *something* to the right.

Right it was.

And he heard flip-flops slapping pavement. Two pair at a run and a third pair much more irregular and farther back.

It was what he needed. Some ancient, long-stored reserve of strength flamed into being, the soldier's training overcoming, even if only for a few moments, the old man's body. He stretched his stride, feeling like he could fly. Angling across the empty street, he leaped for the curb and snagged a foot on it, pitching forward, fighting to get his arms down to break the fall. He landed heavily on one elbow and one knee, knowing immediately that the elbow was a problem, and rolled over twice until he could push himself to his feet with the arm he could still bend, and then he began to move, as much at a limp as a run.

Laughter floated from the boys behind him.

The knee of his pants had torn on impact. There was blood on the cloth, making it stick to his leg. His left elbow was an independent sphere of pain, with a demonic halo of heat around it that seemed to have clamped itself to the middle of his arm and seized his nervous system by sheer force. It squeezed off a machine-gun tangle of agony every time his heart beat. Looking down at it, he saw for the first time that the stinging he'd been feeling in his left forearm was a neat slice, the sleeve of his shirt looking like it had been cut with scissors. The boy he kicked must have gotten to him with a blade as he went down.

Not much farther. He didn't have it in him to go much farther. They could—they could have him.

But the young man inside flared up and said *fuck that,* and Wallace found himself running again, feeling as though he must be leaving red streaks of pain in the air behind him. Doorways and dark windows and occasional fences flowed by, and then, up ahead to the left on his side of the street, he saw light: yellowish, bright, as harsh as a snapped word, but *light.*

A paved area, a parking lot, but not many cars. Instead, knotted wires, carrying stolen electricity direct from the high-voltage lines above, dangled a crop of clear, naked bulbs, spherical as oranges, strung over little stands. A few cars were parked along one edge as though they'd been shoved aside to make room for this little market, just a huddle of carts selling cooked food and produce. Many of them were shutting up, closing the glass doors that kept the flies away, sprinkling water on the charcoal beneath the cooking grates. Among the few remaining shoppers, Wallace saw some *farang*, solitary men as old as he. The vendors had come here as their last stop of the day, hoping to coax the *farang* from their apartments. Old, bent, balding. His age. Left behind when the Golden Mile disappeared.

The business farthest from the street was a glass-sided cart with a long piece of plywood laid across it, perhaps seven or eight feet long, beneath a signboard that said "NOT FAR BAR." Hand-painted below that, in letters of many sizes, was "oNe Bar ComE to YOU!" Four stools had been pulled up to the plywood. Three of them were occupied: a bent-spined man in a blindingly white shirt sitting beside a woman with hair too black even for Thailand, and on the third stool, a plump woman in her late fifties or early sixties, her body popping out of a black cocktail dress that might have fit her twenty years earlier. At one end of the plywood plank, a small boom box was playing "Hotel California."

A portable bar. Wallace had seen a few of these on the sidewalks following the overnight demolition of Sukhumvit Square, but here one was in front of him, as unexpected as an oasis with camels and palm trees. He looked behind him, saw the shoppers thinning and the merchants closing, and went to the empty stool and sat. He couldn't have run another yard if there'd been wolves chasing him.

"Beer Singha," he said, trying to steady his breathing. Now that he was sitting, he felt his legs trembling violently. His left elbow sent up a neural yelp of pain, and the plump woman, who had gotten up to get his beer, took a second look at him and straightened. The powder on her face looked like chalk in the hard light.

"Honey," she said. Her hands indicated the cut shirt, the blood on the cloth. "What happen?"

"Some kids," he said, hearing the quaver in his voice. "It's okay. I just need to sit a minute."

"Poor baby, poor baby," she said. "Kid. Kid no good now. Not same before." She reached into the glass case and pulled out a relatively clean hand towel, then scooped a handful of melting ice and wrapped the towel around it. She lifted the dripping mess, gave it a professional-looking squeeze and held it out. "Here," she said. "For..." She flexed her own left elbow and pointed at it and her forearm with her right hand.

He pressed the wet, cold cloth to his arm, and the fire of pain was banked slightly. A few of the vendors were stretching up, holding towels or potholders to unscrew the bulbs over their carts. The kids were nowhere in sight.

"You say kid..." the woman in black said. She popped the cap off a Singha. At her end of the bar was a big Chinese cleaver on a circular wooden cutting board, piled with limes. She grabbed the cleaver and expertly sliced a lime, then remembered to ask, "Glass?"

He shook his head.

"Kid how old? How many?" She dropped the lime slice back onto the board, thunked the cleaver's edge into the wood, wiped the bottle dry and put it in front of him. Then she hoisted herself onto the stool beside him and rested her hand on his thigh in the eternal gesture of bar girls everywhere.

"Three. Not kids, really. In their twenties. Smoking…" He mimed the little pipe with his left hand.

"*Yaa baa*," she said. She nodded. "I see before. Bangkok now no good."

A fat Thai with a Chinese face waddled out of the darkness. Behind him Wallace saw an aluminum lawn chaise with a blanket on it. "We close soon," the man said. "Order last drink, please."

"Aaaaahhhhhh," the man with the bent spine said. "I'll quit now." He put a couple of bills down and dropped some coins on top and pushed the stool back. Standing, he was no taller than he was sitting, his back as crooked as a question mark. "You," he said to Wallace. "You oughta see a doctor. That arm's busted."

"I think so, too," Wallace said.

"Little shits around here," the other man said. "Know we're old. Know what days the pension checks arrive. Little fuckers. Oughta carry a gun if you're gonna come here."

"I won't be back," Wallace said.

"Smart guy. Get that arm looked at, hear?" To the woman beside him, he said, "Coming?"

"I go with you?" the woman said, doing her best to look surprised and pleased.

"Sure, sure. We talk money later, okay?"

"No problem." She grabbed a tiny purse and darted a quick, victorious glance at the woman beside Wallace, then took the bent man's arm, and the two of them headed for the street.

"Why you come?" asked the woman in the tight dress.

"Golden Mile," Wallace said.

"Ah," she said, her face softening. "Golden Mile, yes. Very good."

"You know a girl named Jah?" Wallace asked.

He got a moment of silence as she gnawed her lower lip. "I know many Jah."

"At Thai Heaven."

"No," she said. "I no work Thai Heaven. Work Tidbit Bar."

"Mmmm," Wallace said and knocked back half of the beer. With the bottle halfway down, he froze.

She followed his gaze and saw the three of them in a loose triangle at the edge of the lot. She pointed at them with a tilt of her chin. "Them?"

"Yes," Wallace said.

"You stay," the plump woman said, and faster than he would have thought possible, she was at the end of the bar and had grabbed the cleaver. Raising it high in the air, she ran toward them, small steps because of the tight dress, but a run nevertheless. The boys stepped back, and when she showed no sign of slowing, they turned and retreated out of sight, back up the street. The woman with the cleaver followed.

His hand trembled as he downed the rest of the beer.

She trotted back into sight, hair slightly disarranged, but with a smile on her face. She sank the cleaver's edge into the side of the cutting board and said, "They go, but maybe still close. You pay, you come with me. I take you home. We go." She waited, not sitting, until he'd put the money on the plywood, and then laced her left arm through his uninjured right and led him toward the street, in the direction opposite the one the boys had taken.

She wore a light floral perfume, something that made Wallace think of a place he and his friends had played each spring, in the hills above Carlsbad, California, slopes of blue lupine and the eye-ringing orange of California poppies tumbling down to the hard bright sun-wrinkles of the sea. Looking for the secret messages they had left there the previous fall, when the hills grew dry and prickly. Answers to questions they'd asked each other, maps to things they'd hidden.

Maps.

They were on the sidewalk now, the lights receding behind them as they moved parallel to New Petchburi Road. In the moments he'd been sitting, Wallace's knee had stiffened, and he was limping. He said, "How can you take me home? You don't know where I live."

"No problem," she said. "I take you where you can get taxi, get tuk-tuk. Take you home."

The shophouse, he thought. *No, no, that's not right.*

"Have taxi up here," she said. "Come little bit more." They were beneath a street light, her face suddenly blossoming from the dark.

"Jah?" Wallace said, and then she looked over her shoulder and he heard them.

"In here." She shoved him into a narrow space between two buildings, half-illuminated by the street light, with chunks of rubble underfoot. She pushed him in front of her, and then a blue flame ignited ahead of them—the boy with the crimp in his head—and the other two came into the space behind them, the woman backing away, looking from face to face.

He'd turned to face the two who had just come in when he heard the grit of a step behind him and then something enormously hard slammed the side of his head. His vision flared orange as the thing hit him again, banging the other side of his head against the wall of the building. He was sliding, sliding somewhere, feeling a rough surface against his arm and shoulder, and then something rose up from below, very fast, and struck him on the underside of the chin, and his head snapped back so hard he thought he heard something break.

The woman was screaming in Thai, sounding not frightened but furious, and one of the boys barked a string of syllables like rocks, and she fell silent. Someone kicked him in the ribs, but he barely felt it.

There were stars up there at the top of the narrow canyon between the buildings. He hadn't seen stars often in Bangkok.

A hand under his head, lifting it up, putting it on something soft, her leg. The woman, looking down at him, fat and powdered, her face shining with sweat. He saw the eyes, the bones, the skin—and the fat and the years melted away, and the corners of her mouth curled up, and the lacquered hair fell loose and long, and he said, "Jah."

"I'm here, *teerak*," she said. "You okay now, I'm here."

"I looked for you," Wallace said. The world dipped sharply down for an instant, everything going sideways, but he forced it back the way it should have been.

"You found me," she said. "You found me." She wiped his face gently with her hand. "Always I wait for you."

Someone had a hand in his pocket but when Wallace looked down the world tilted again, and this time it kept going and the street light went down like the sun. He was alone in an empty room, the walls rushing away from him, the space growing bigger and emptier and darker until the only light was him, whatever *he* was, a sharp point of white light, narrowing to a pinprick, and he said again, "Jah," and the light blinked out.

"Who's Jah?" asked the boy with the crimped head, fanning the wad of bills.

"How would I know?" the woman said. "Some *teerak* from a hundred years ago. Why'd you hit him so hard?"

"He hurt Beer's leg," said the boy with the crimped head.

"Pussy," the woman said. "Hurt by an old man." She eased Wallace's head off her leg and lowered it softly to the pavement. His eyes were open, looking straight up. "Give me a hand."

The boy called Beer limped forward and helped her up. Instantly, she was slapping him, hard, and then she clawed his face and backed off. "All you had to do was take the money," she said. "Make me look like a victim and take the money. You *stupid* boy."

She lowered her head to look again at Wallace. She said, "I liked him."

Thirty seconds passed in silence. No one even shuffled his feet. The woman extended her hand, and the boy with the crimped head passed her a tight crumple of bills. She tucked them into the front of her dress, brushed cement dust from the black fabric and leaned down to straighten Wallace's shirt, which had been pulled up when he slid down the wall. Then she smoothed the long gray hair from his forehead. The boys filed out, leaving her there, her eyes on Wallace's face.

"Long time ago," she said to no one, not even knowing she was speaking English. "Long time ago, I think you was hansum man."

Timothy Hallinan

Timothy Hallinan is an American thriller writer, based in Southern California and Southeast Asia. In the 1990s, Hallinan created the erudite private eye Simeon Grist, who appeared in a total of six novels, all set in Los Angeles. Since publication in 2007, his second series, set in Bangkok, has received critical acclaim. Tim has lived off and on in Thailand since the early 1980s. His Bangkok-based series features a rough-travel writer named Philip ("Poke") Rafferty, who has settled in the Thai capital and is in the process of trying to cobble together a family comprising Rose, the former go-go dancer he loves, and a precocious street urchin named Miaow. His newest series, which begins with the 2010 novel *Crashed*, features a burglar named Junior Bender who moonlights as a private eye for crooks.

Daylight

Alex Kerr

All the witnesses agreed. The victim, an upcountry
visitor to Bangkok of no particular importance, had died
by stabbing on the BTS platform at three in the afternoon. He was thirty-eight years old, was named Kaew,
had worked in a motorcycle repair shop in Khon Kaen
and had died from stab wounds to his legs, abdomen
and lungs. After a thorough autopsy had determined
the cause of death, the family had collected the body
and taken it back to Khon Kaen for cremation.

Including Kaew's brother Nop, there had been
about thirty witnesses on the crowded platform that
day, of whom six had come forward to the police.
Two young office ladies had been quick enough to
actually record the incident on their cell phone video
cameras, and the images were crystal clear because it
had been a bright, sunny afternoon. They had all
pinpointed the same person as the murderer, who
had been duly questioned by the police.

At this point the rather thin file ended. An open
and closed case, really. I put it down on the desk,

looked out the window at Bangkok's rows of white skyscrapers stretching off under the pale light of early morning and wondered why this would interest anyone. It must have been a very slow day in New York because my editor had somehow become aware of a murder on the Skytrain in Bangkok and asked me to look into it.

I live for the night. Bangkok, for me, begins at about four in the afternoon and only comes alive around midnight. So it was a grim moment when the phone rang at 5:00 a.m. with a sharp Brooklyn accent demanding that I get up immediately and submit a full report to New York within twelve hours.

Staying up all night and going to sleep when the sun rises is fine, but dawn is truly depressing when seen from the wrong end. A few cups of coffee later, the first rays of sunlight were striking the tops of the skyscrapers, and I was feeling a bit better. I reviewed the file again and then noticed the dissonant note that should have been obvious from the beginning: the suspect hadn't been arrested. More strangely, his name was never mentioned at any point in any of the reports. A police cover-up? But if so, why, in a case involving someone of no particular importance? Or was it just a slip-up in the paperwork? Well, New York needed something fast, and I had just a day to find some angle on this case.

Time for breakfast. In the *soi* next to mine I used to enjoy walking past a charming but decrepit old wooden house intriguingly overgrown with huge vines. Then they tore it down and replaced it with a sleek white apartment building and opened an all-day breakfast café in an airy, glassy room on the first floor. All I had to do was to bear the morning heat for a few minutes as I slipped through the back streets to this little hideaway. There, surrounded by the French models who stay at the apartments in the upper floors, I could sit and surf the internet on the café's Wi-Fi. If lucky, I'd find the missing pieces of this case online before finishing the last piece of toast.

But here I drew a blank. Usually murder cases get some mention in the news, often complete with lurid photos of gruesomely wounded corpses spread across the front page of daily newspapers like *Thai Rath*. In this case there was only silence. The sources and pages that should have covered the case just weren't there. It was as if a hole had opened up in the internet and swallowed the whole incident. Well, the internet in Bangkok is like that. There are gaps, and you get used to it.

Curiosity piqued, I made my way back to my *soi*, now palpably a few degrees hotter, the tarmac simmering under the morning sun. I reentered my office with a sense of unease. Usually an hour or two on the internet is enough to satisfy New York. This time I had the foreboding that this case would actually involve some work.

First, some phone calls. The obvious person to start with would be Nop, Kaew's brother. Nop had suffered minor cuts while trying to protect his brother, and after being treated in Bangkok had returned to Khon Kaen to recover.

I considered. Yes, one could catch a flight to Khon Kaen and get back in twelve hours. But I'm lazy. I've become a true Bangkokian in that I tend to feel that the civilized world falls away somewhere along the Bangna highway. There's town, and there's the long hot trek to a resort somewhere. Better to stay in my air-conditioned office. That's what telephones are for.

It was easy enough to reach Nop. Although a Khon Kaen farmer, he too had a cell phone, making him just as accessible as someone in Bangkok. And then began one of those baffling conversations you can sometimes have in Thailand.

"Do you know who killed Kaew?

"Of course I know."

"Who is it?"

"You should ask someone about that."

"You mean the police? They're not talking."

"I guess they wouldn't."

"Is there anything you can tell me?"

"Just talk to the people you know. And then you'll know."

And with that, Nop hung up.

Nop was trying to tell me something, but who in the world would "people that I know" be? All I could think of were the people who had been at the scene. Best start with the six official witnesses. When I took another look at the files, the police had duly noted the names and contact numbers of the two girls who had taken the videos.

So an hour later I found myself eating lunch with two giggly office girls in one of those huge food courts on the top of a department store downtown. By now it was the noon-time rush hour, and bathed in the all-pervading glow of fluorescent lights, and surrounded by the coming and going of people clinking trays and plastic plates, it didn't seem like a place to unravel a murder.

It took a while to get the girls, dressed smartly in red and green, to stop smiling and giggling out of embarrassment at being accosted by a foreigner. But finally they calmed down and pulled out their cell phones. Sure enough, the videos they'd taken were still there, and I could see the whole tragedy unfold, from the knife attack on Kaew to the moment when the police rushed up and apprehended the suspect. He looked to be about forty, was clean-cut, but neither in his clothing nor speech seemed to be anyone of importance. He was defiant. "I had to kill Kaew," he declared. "There was no other choice."

"What do you think he meant by that?" I asked. The girls wanted me to help decide which of their two cell phones had taken the best video. We watched again. The red-dress girl thought her

Nokia version was clearer and the colors brighter, and I had to agree. But the green-dress girl insisted her Samsung sound quality had been better. Off they went in high spirits.

I still didn't know the name of the suspect, or his motive, but one thing that came across was that this wasn't a crime of passion. It was planned; it was serious. Maybe this was a gang killing. "I had to kill him"—that's the sort of thing they say in gang vendettas. I wondered if Kaew was perhaps mixed up in drugs. There must have been lots of money, and maybe family pride was involved.

The girls had let me download their videos onto my computer. If I watched the videos closely enough, there might be some clue. So, seated in the vast food court, I looked again.

I noticed that there were faces in the crowd that I could recognize. I *knew* these people. Was that the lady who sells fried chicken at the corner? That man wearing a striped shirt—he lives on my street. We've talked in the café. As happens at a moment like this, my mind ran amok. I went from seeing one or two people that I thought I recognized to where suddenly every single person in those videos looked familiar. I couldn't place them exactly, but I could swear that I'd seen them all.

Obviously, that was impossible. I decided I must be suffering from an overdose of morning light. Maybe it was the fluorescent glare and the tray-clinking crowds that were making me dizzy. Too many photons striking the retina at an early hour. It's not healthy.

I stumbled out onto the open street, baking under the full blaze of the afternoon sun. Cars crawled sluggishly along clogged avenues, while busy pedestrians veered around me on the crumbling sidewalk. A vendor tried hard to sell me a wooden frog whose serrated back he stroked with a little stick, producing a croaking sound. I've seen that frog a hundred times, and it came as such a relief, a return to normalcy, that for a moment I even considered buying it. I was back to Bangkok as I knew it.

But no, something had *changed*. It had happened while I was watching the videos in the food court. I had the feeling I had become a cell phone recording an incident that had happened or was about to happen, but the color and sound quality were not as good as either a Nokia or a Samsung. The light was too bright, the sounds muffled. Bangkok hustled by, in all its chaos and color, but I was missing a key ingredient. People on the street knew something I didn't. Maybe Kaew's killing, although he was a person of no importance, really did have some importance.

It was time to call Evelyn Xu. She's beautiful, goes to all the parties and is infinitely savvy about the city and full of good gossip. Why didn't I think of her before? But first I needed to get off the street and sit down. It wasn't long, of course, before I found a Starbucks, which was perfect because in its bland international chicness, it erased Bangkok for a moment. In here there were no gangs, no mysterious money, no Kaews or Nops. Just tall or grande.

"Evelyn, what do you know about the murder that happened last week on the Skytrain?" I asked. "You mean Kaew?" she replied. I was shocked that she was familiar with the name. How did Evelyn know about it? "Everyone knows about Kaew," she said dismissively. In that case, did she know the name of the suspect? "Well, you hear stories. But it's useless to even think about it," she replied. "Anyway, there's going to be the most incredible party this weekend. The top ten Japanese fashion brands are doing a joint event, spread over ten penthouses across the city. You really should go."

"Wait a minute." There seemed no sense to all this mystification if everyone already knew about Kaew. "Can't you help me at all?" At this point Evelyn drew a breath and said simply: "Just talk to the people you know. And then you'll know."

My heart turned to ice. It was exactly what Nop had told me.

"Even if you don't want to go round to all the penthouses," she burbled, "come along with me and we can see the top three."

"Okay, thanks, Evelyn."

It was now three in the afternoon. The most dreadful time of day in Bangkok. In other parts of the world, the stroke of midnight would be the witching hour, the moment when ghastly things happen. Here, it's 3:00 p.m.

Bangkok lore is replete with scary spirits, *phii*, who haunt the night alleys with disgusting entrails dangling, mouths foaming, tails flailing. But these *phii* have nothing on the great invisible Spirit of the Afternoon, who descends at 3:00 p.m., lowering her smoggy wings over the city, siphoning away the oxygen and disturbing people's hearts and minds. A sluggish reptile that needs to bask in the sunlight for a while before she musters the energy to move, she wakes in the morning, but only goes hunting in earnest in the afternoon. Traffic grinds to a halt; clocks slow; business deals flounder; marriages grow stale; the heat reaches its unbearable apex. Taxi drivers talk too much and drive recklessly. People like Kaew die. Not a good time to go out in the sun.

Then I caught sight of Ajarn Jaa sitting in the corner. An influential academic, Jaa is one of those daunting Thai figures that one knows but, despite a welcoming smile, hesitates to become too familiar with. We bump into each other at the press club, and he always has something erudite to say. Jaa dwells in a knowledgeable heaven of his own. But I thought: "Here's someone I know! Isn't that what Nop and Evelyn have been telling me? 'Talk to people you know.'"

I grabbed another iced cappuccino and sat down, uninvited, at Jaa's table. He smiled welcomingly. After what seemed like an hour of pleasantries, I finally broached the question: "Ajarn, do you know anything about the murder that took place last week on the Skytrain of a man named Kaew?" This time I hit the jackpot.

Jaa was brimming with information. Yes, it was drugs, and money, lots of money, some of it counterfeit from North Korea. Jaa even knew about Kaew's brother Nop, who was in deep as well, so it would be best to avoid him. In fact, Kaew's whole family is involved in criminal networks. Jaa appeared to have made quite a study of the case. He regaled me with story after story, practically a genealogy of Kaew and his renegade clan from Khon Kaen. As he spoke, the pieces fell together, and I began to see the logic of the thing. Given a background like this, it's surprising that someone hadn't got Kaew even earlier. As for the drugs and money—well, in Bangkok that's hardly news. It was a prosaic case after all.

"It's been good chatting with you," Jaa remarked, and granting me the most refined of *wais*, he whiffed out the Starbucks door and was gone. I stayed behind, delighted at my good fortune in getting some real information, until it hit me: Jaa never had given me the name of the killer.

Jaa had provided motive for a case of crime and vendetta. But after all that factual input, the identity of the man who stabbed Kaew stubbornly refused to reveal itself. The question that I started with in the morning remained unanswered. By this time it was 4:00 p.m., and although the day was still bright and hot, I had no choice but to exit Starbucks and brave the crowded Skytrain home. In Thai the words for "four o'clock" and "five o'clock" are *sii mong yen* and *haa mong yen*, "four drumbeats cool" and "five drumbeats cool," meaning presumably the cool of the afternoon, but it never made sense to me. There's nothing cool about a Bangkok afternoon, except the icy chill of the Skytrain itself, which makes the heat seem even more oppressive when you exit.

Steeped in thought, I walked down the steps from the Skytrain and then stopped in my tracks, the breath literally sucked from my lungs.

There she was. The lady selling fried chicken. She was a witness, and I'd seen her in the video. Now here was a case of asking someone that I know. I bought some fried chicken and thought about how I could bring this matter up. I'm well aware that directness is never the right way in Thailand, but I had to ask her. As she began chopping up the chicken, I blurted it out: "What did you see at the Skytrain last week?"

Through the oily steam billowing from her woks, I saw something in her eyes. Nop had been noncommittal. Evelyn had focused on her parties. The girls in red and green had seen the whole incident as a photo op. Ajarn Jaa had been caught up in the complexity of his theories. But this woman was afraid. In her eyes I saw a deep and implacable fear. "I wasn't there," she stammered. As she handed me a little plastic bag of chicken and rice, she whispered, "You'd better go home."

There was clearly no point in pressing further. I thought: "I'd better take her words at face value. It's time to go home." In any case it was almost five o'clock, and soon New York would be on the phone demanding a response.

As I entered my building, I recognized someone seated in the lobby. It was the man in the striped shirt. He reintroduced himself as Khun Jaeng, a Thai banker. His condo was a few hundred meters down the *soi*. Could he come up to my apartment to talk?

He looked so proper, I felt it would be rude to refuse. You never know what trouble an act of rudeness could later cause you. So I invited him up.

We sat down in the living room, the late afternoon sun slanting through the windows and beaming through glasses of iced tea on the glass table between us. Pleasantries were exchanged. "I see you sometimes at the café, and since I live on the same *soi*, it's a pity we haven't had a chance to meet properly," Khun Jaeng opened.

It was hard to focus on the conversation. Why was this person in my home? The light shining from behind Jaeng's chair fell straight into my eyes, dazzling, disorienting. I had a report to file soon with very little real information to offer, and in New York they would not be amused.

Into my head flashed a scene from the old French novel *Thaïs*. A hermit has been meditating for decades in a desert hut, and every evening six black jackals come and sit outside. One night he has an unsettling dream, and when he awakes the next morning, he finds one little jackal sitting inside his tent. He knows then that outside forces have penetrated his magic ring.

The Phii of the Afternoon had breached my defenses. She had forced herself in and was shining light into a space usually shadowed.

The Phii of the Night drape themselves in outlandish costumes and go out and do a little hooting and grimacing, which scares the good people of the city as they walk dark byways. But after a few hours of haunting, these *phii* retire and you rarely see them again. The Phii of the Afternoon, on the other hand, once she's entered your home, never goes away. I realized with finality that she would be waiting for me when I arose the next day. And the day after.

I wrenched myself back to Khun Jaeng, who was rambling on about our *soi*, the traffic, the breakfast menu at the café. Then finally: "I hear you're investigating the incident on the Skytrain last week," he remarked.

How on earth could he have known? But of course, he was a witness. He's mixed up in this very intimately. The look in the eyes of the chicken lady still fresh in my mind, I proceeded with caution.

"The incident?"

"Yes, the killing of that man Kaew. We know you're interested in that."

"*We?*"

"Well, you know, we all saw it. We know what really happened. You never will."

I glanced down at my watch. It was 5:00 p.m. Like a Zen adept who experiences enlightenment in the instant when his master asks where he had set his shoes, at the words "You never will," I suddenly saw it. It was so simple.

Khun Jaeng was right.

I would never know. Looking back, this had been clear right at the beginning. An epiphany, it made sense of those Bangkok streets I'd walked through earlier that seemed to have mysteriously changed.

Mundane practicality reasserted itself. What could I tell New York? They wanted facts. With a jolt I realized that Khun Jaeng was still seated in the living room, looking at me expectantly with a glass of iced tea in his hand.

"You're quite right," I assured him. And like a murderer who's keeping a body in the closet but hopes the police won't open that particular panel, I slowly edged Khun Jaeng to the exit, hoping he would ask no more questions. Thankfully he didn't. More *wais*.

Finally I was alone. The phone rang. It was New York. "About the Skytrain murder…" I began, but my editor had no time for that.

"A bomb went off in New Delhi. Who cares about the Bangkok Skytrain?"

"You asked me to look into it."

"You know we only run that Thai stuff as a sop to people planning trips there. It's time to focus on serious news. See if you can find a Southeast Asia angle to the India story. Otherwise, never mind. We'll call you when something comes up." And she was off the line.

It was six. The setting sun was blowing huge orange and purple balloons across the Bangkok skyline. New York didn't need the story after all, and what a relief. The Bangkok night was coming on, and the Phii of the Afternoon was visibly losing energy. The snake had struck, was digesting her meal and would soon curl up and go to sleep. Leaving the night open and free.

I knew I would never again speak of Kaew to anybody. Which was fine because, after all, he was a person of no particular importance.

Alex Kerr

Alex Kerr (born 1952) is an American writer based in Japan and Thailand. He is well known for his book *Lost Japan* (1994), which describes the changes he witnessed in the country where he has lived on and off for decades since childhood. Alex originally wrote *Lost Japan* in Japanese, for which he was the first foreigner to be awarded the Shincho Gakugei Literature Prize for the best work of non-fiction published in Japan. His later book *Dogs and Demons* (2002), addresses issues of environmental degradation and loss of native culture in the wake of modernization and Westernization. Since the 1980's, Alex has made Bangkok his second home, establishing in 2005 the Origin Program to introduce traditional Thai arts to foreign visitors. His most recent work is *Bangkok Found* (2010), which explores the cultural themes of his Japan writing within the Thai context.

Death of a Legend

Dean Barrett

His dark brown hands working the cleaning rod were large. By Thai standards they were huge. Stubby and rough. But not calloused. And despite their size his finger had no problem slipping inside the trigger guard and working the Smith and Wesson revolver when occasion demanded it. It was what he did for a living. And he was good at what he did.

But what struck you on seeing him for the first time was his overall size. Something about an Asian male of six foot, two inches, with lots of bulk—far more functional muscle than fat—made you either take a second look or look away so as not to draw his attention. But unless he had a contract to eliminate you, you had nothing to worry about. He was the type of hit man who never shot or beat up anyone or even raised his voice without being hired to do so. Using his talent for free would have been anathema to him. And that's why, despite his nearly unbroken string of victories against better known opponents, he had left the Muay Thai ring forever. Why kick people senseless if there was no money in it? The only thing he still had from those days was a slight scar over his left eye and a damaged elbow that ached during the rainy season. And the tattoo of a scorpion on his broad back.

He was casually dressed in an open shirt, which revealed a thick neck without wrinkles, although he was already well into his late forties. He had served a few years inside Bang Kwang prison for one mistake or another, but those were the days of his youth, and those days were over. Now, when he received a call for his services, he spent days, even weeks, surveying the scene, checking out the person he was to hit—or in his lingo, the *poo rap*, "receiver." He never asked what the receiver had done to deserve to be on the receiving end of his talent; that wasn't his business. His business, as the *poo hai*, "provider," was to do the job and leave the scene without being identified, much less caught. And despite increasingly difficult and dangerous assignments, he had never failed.

The living room he was in was on the third floor of a run-down apartment building in a section of Bangkok infested with freelance Thai hookers, elderly, Viagra-fuelled johns and filthy short-time hotels. The room was permeated with the stale smell of some spicy northeastern Thai dish. But he was from a village near Petchaburi, a town known for producing excellent hit men. And even though he had fled the province in his teens, he still favored the unique cuisine his mother could make from the area's plentiful sugar palm fruits.

A colorful but clichéd painting of a Thai village scene hung on a wall. A village not unlike the one he grew up in—except the painting had left out the poverty, the drunkards, the anger, the petty feuds and the feeling of confinement. And yet even the amateurish rendition of a Thai village made him nostalgic for the way things had been. Before his first hit.

The room's sofa was worn. Everything was worn, old, second-hand, shabby, used up. A cheap wooden statue of a Buddha in meditation was on a shelf above a cracked oval wall mirror, which reflected the poverty of the room. But there was no dust or dirt; it was just shabby. Someone lived here. Someone who had probably been paid a few thousand baht to make themselves scarce for a few hours.

A thick white bath towel and a clean set of shirt and trousers had been neatly folded and placed on top of an out-of-date television set. A narrow hallway led into the darkness of unseen inner rooms. The venetian blinds on the only window of the room were dust-covered and stained with yellow spots. They were tilted downward, and a few streaks of late-afternoon light spilled out across the table beside his glass of Mekong whiskey.

He paused to take a drink and then again worked the cleaning rod into the weapon, meticulously and without hurry. Steel cleaning rods and small white cotton cleaning patches were spread out neatly on the sports page of a Thai language newspaper. Beside the paper were his gun-cleaning kit and a can of gun conditioner oil. And five bullets. He would occasionally hold the revolver up to the ceiling's old-fashioned circular fluorescent light and check the barrel or cylinder for any buildup of debris or sign of rust. Regardless of what he saw, he would replace the patch with a clean one, sparingly spotted with oil, and clean again. A friend of his who had been a monk for years had told him that what he was doing wasn't really cleaning the gun, that for him it had become a meditative experience. The big man had liked the phrase and remembered it.

The knock on the door was tentative and soft. The man continued to clean. His voice was rasping and gruff, he figured from the years when he still smoked. "Yeah."

After a pause, the knock came again. Only slightly louder.

"Yeah!"

The door opened slowly and a thin, young Thai man entered cautiously. He was in his early to mid-twenties and wore an expensive street jacket over a long-sleeved shirt and well pressed trousers. His leather shoes looked as if they'd been spit-shined. His complexion was several shades whiter than that of the big man. He attempted to affect a cocky exterior but his nervousness was obvious. He stared at the big man for several seconds and then closed the door and looked around the room.

"You left the door unlocked?"

"If you say so."

"What if it had been him?"

For the first time the man in the chair glanced up to look at the boy. Then he continued cleaning his weapon. "Him?"

"The guy we've been hired to hit. He's a legend!"

"Legends die, kid. Like anything else."

"But he might have come here early and—"

"And what?" For a few seconds the man stopped cleaning and locked eyes with the boy. Then he resumed cleaning. "Don't worry, kid, he's known to be punctual."

The boy hesitated and then walked to the man and held out his hand. The man ignored it.

"I'm Sombat Ti—"

"Don't tell me your name. Don't ever tell me your name. How long you been in this business?"

"Uh… Lo-long time…"

"So how long you been here?"

"A while. Wichai hire you?"

"Yeah, Wichai."

"What'd he tell you?"

"About what?

"About the hit!"

"Just that the guy does what we do. And that he's the best."

"What do we do?"

The boy threw his shoulders back and began strutting as he spoke. "You know. Eliminate obstacles for people. Settle disputes. Solve problems. Permanently... Like when I did the Kaeochart hit."

"*You* did the Kaeochart hit?"

"Yeah, I did the hit. You heard about it, huh?"

"Kid, everybody in the business has heard about the Kaeochart hit. Right in the middle of Lumpini Park. I heard the shooter got off the motorcycle, brushed past the guy's bodyguards, shot his target, walked casually back to his bike and took off. He was staring at them the whole time. Bodyguards were too scared to react."

"Yeah. Yeah, that's the way it was. Cool and daring." The boy stopped to preen himself a bit in the mirror and stared at the big man's reflection. "But the guy we're waiting for pissed Wichai off."

"That right?"

"Yeah. I don't know what. But if Wichai wants him dead, he must have fucked up big time. So Wichai wants it done and done right. That's why he sent me." The boy checked his watch. He suddenly spotted the clothes on the TV set. He held up the towel. "What's with the clothes and towel? ... Oh. That's good. That's really good."

"What's good, kid?"

"I can see from the way you're cleaning your gun. You value cleanliness. So you brought clean clothes, just in case you get blood on what you're wearing."

The big man stared at the boy and said nothing.

"Or maybe it's like a spiritual thing. You change clothes after a hit and throw away the old clothes. Shed the old skin. Start out fresh. Right?"

The big man took another hit of Mekong. "If I were you, I'd clean my weapon."

The boy reached inside his jacket and, not without difficulty, pulled out a semi-automatic. "Don't worry. Mine is always clean." He popped out the clip and then slid it back in. "And ready."

"It better be. This guy is the best there is. Like you said, a legend."

The boy replaced his gun in his shoulder holster inside his jacket. "Yeah? So how come I didn't recognize him in the picture Manny showed me?"

"Kid, when you're recognized in this business, you're dead. And I doubt the legend ever allowed any recent photo to be taken."

The boy continued to walk about. "What a dump. Whose apartment is this, anyway?"

"I couldn't tell you, kid. It's safe enough for the hit. That's all we need to know."

"Well, I know he thinks he's coming here for a meeting. Wichai told him it's a meeting to plan a hit." The boy slammed his fist into his palm. "Hah! But what he doesn't know is *he's* the target. We're the hitters and he's the hittee! This should be fun."

The big man gave him a look, saying nothing.

The boy looked at his watch. "Shouldn't he be here by now?"

"He'll be here. And shouldn't you be sitting down somewhere by now?"

The boy walked toward the man and stopped just a foot away. His hand reached out near the man's gun. "Hey! Tha—"

The big man quickly and expertly moved behind the boy, throwing one arm around his neck and holding a knife at his throat.

"I... I was only going to say Ampol won at Lumpini again. It's... it's there. In your newspaper. I mean, motherfucker, he's practically an old man and he's still fighting."

The man looked toward the newspaper and understood his mistake. In his day Ampol had been one of the best Muay Thai fighters he had ever fought. It was Ampol's incredibly fast mid-air elbow strike which had scarred his face and dropped him. One of the big man's few defeats in the ring.

He released the boy, replaced his knife in his belt and sat down. He reached into his gun kit and withdrew a silicone gun cloth. He began wiping down his revolver. "Sorry, kid. I thought... You know."

The boy stared at the big man. "That hurt! We're on the same side, right?"

"You been in this business a long time, right?"

"Yeah, that's right."

"Lots of hits, right?"

"Yeah. That's right."

"So how come you talk so much?"

The boy stared at the man, his expression a cross between shame and anger, and sat down on the sofa.

"... How come you still use a revolver? You only get five shots with what you got."

"Had a semi-automatic jam on me once. Almost got me killed."

"I got thirteen rounds. And one in the chamber."

"Doesn't matter how many rounds you got if your weapon jams. You're dead. You die because you're semi jams, you'll end up the wrong kind of legend. "

"Don't worry about me. I'm gonna be the right kind of legend. The biggest there ever was. I'm gonna be the best! A guy's name is what counts, and people are gonna say my name with respect."

The boy pointed his finger toward the room's only floor lamp and pretended to fire.

"Bad-ass, huh?"

"Damn right!"

"And you'll get top dollar?"

"Fuckin' A!"

The boy took out a pack of cigarettes, placed one between his lips and struck a match.

"This is a no-smoking area."

"You're joking, right?"

"I don't mind dying quick with a round through the heart, but I'm not lying in a hospital bed coughing my lungs out."

The boy hesitated and then angrily snubbed the match out. He muttered a swear word under his breath. He tried to sit still but was too restless and fidgety.

Footsteps sounded in the hallway. The kid drew his gun and jumped up. The man continued cleaning as before. The footsteps faded. The man glanced up at the boy. The boy, embarrassed, put his gun away and sat down.

"Shouldn't we at least lock the door? I mean, he could barge in on us and take us out before we could react... You just gonna keep cleanin' that thing?"

"Two rules, kid. One, respect your weapon. Two, respect the intelligence of your opponent."

"That's why we should lock the door."

"No. That's why we should leave it unlocked."

"Man, I just hope—"

The big man suddenly stared into the inner hallway of the apartment and held up his hand. "Shhh!"

"What?"

"You hear anything?"

The boy jumped up awkwardly. "No... I don't know."

"Maybe I should have checked the other rooms."

"You didn't check the apartment?"

"The front door was locked when I got here." The big man shrugged. "I just thought—"

"You dog's ass!"

The boy pulled out his weapon and rushed from the room. The big man watched him enter the narrow inner hallway and disappear. The man quickly placed all five bullets in his cylinder, snapped it shut and placed his revolver in a belt holster. He rose and stood to the side of the hallway where the boy wouldn't be able to spot him in time.

He could hear the panic in the boy's voice. "Motherfucker! Motherfucker!"

The boy rushed into the living room, gun in hand. The man drew his own gun.

"There's a body in the bathtub! There's blood all over the fuckin' place! You hear me? There's a body in the—"

In one fast, smooth movement, the man lifted the boy's gun from his hand as he smashed his own gun down on the back of the boy's head. The boy fell to his knees, stunned by the blow.

"Don't move."

The man placed the boy's gun in his own belt and checked his body for other weapons. The boy held the back of his head with both hands.

"Jesus Christ! My head! Are you crazy?"

The man finished patting him down. He found no other weapons.

"Okay, I get it. He came early. You wasted him before I got here. You want to keep all the money, right? Okay. You earned it, so keep it! It's yours. I'll tell Wichai I got here too late. You hadda do the job yourself. Just let me go!"

The man walked behind him and placed the muzzle of his revolver flush against the back of the boy's head. "You still don't get it, do you, kid? The man in the bathtub was the man you were supposed to meet."

"... The who?"

"I'm the legend."

The boy started to turn his head, but the man pushed the gun harder. "Don't turn around, kid."

"How did you..."

"I warned you: always respect the intelligence of your opponent. You don't get to be a legend by falling into traps. I'm not the hittee." He cocked the hammer of his revolver. *You* are."

"Don't! Please!"

"Okay, kid, here's how it works. You tried a hit; it backfired. But nothing personal, right? No need for you to suffer. So, I'm going to send a round into your brain. It's the fastest way to get your body to shut down. But, even then, your heart will most likely keep pumping for a few minutes. Problem is, it'll be pumping the blood *out* of your system. Like the plug's been pulled, and the heart's now working against itself. A brainless muscle if ever there was one, huh? Then your body temperature falls and your system begins shutting down. Clinical death. Biological death. End of story..."

"Please, no! Don't kill me! I can pay you. Just take my wallet! I'll—"

"Stop crying, kid. It doesn't help. But I'll tell you something. You know what I noticed in this business, kid? Some guys die with their eyes open, and some die with their eyes shut. I wondered about that for years. Then I decided that either was acceptable. There isn't any god that cares one way or the other. But the guy with his eyes open? I'd say he's more dead than the guy with his eyes shut. Which are you gonna be, kid? Open or shut?"

"Don't kill me! Please! I'll pay you whatever you want!"

"Kid, don't take it so hard. Like I said, it's nothing personal. But if I don't waste you now, you might come after me. Who knows? You might get lucky."

"No! I wouldn't. I swear it. I wouldn't dare!"

"No? A man with all your hits might dare anything. After all, you did the Kaeochart hit."

"I never hit anybody! I never killed anybody! This is my first time. I just wanted to be like my uncle. He was in the business for years. I just wanted to be like him! Please, don't! I'll never come after you!"

"I believe you, kid. 'Cause, you see, *I* did the Kaeochart hit."

"Oh, I—look, mister, please!"

"You had it right, except you weren't there to see my semi jam up on me. I had to use the backup revolver. That's why I won't touch a semi-automatic again."

"Look, I swear I—"

"But it's like this. You being an amateur makes it even worse. Somebody teams you up with a guy like me, a pro, and you could accidentally get the pro killed by doing something stupid. I can't allow that to happen."

The boy's sobbing grew louder. His voice broke. "No! I swear. I don't want to kill anybody. I'll never do this again. Nobody will die because of me. Please don't kill me! Please! Take my wallet! Just let me go!"

"... If, *if* I let you go, how do I know you'll keep your word?"

"Mister, I swear to you! If I ever try this again, you come after me and kill me, Okay? I just want out. Please!"

The big man slowly let the hammer down. "Okay, kid. That'll be the deal. You try another hit, I'll hear about it. And I'll put a bullet through you."

"Yes! Yes! But you won't have to. I swear it. Please!"

"I told you to stop crying. ... You piss your pants?"

"...Yes."

"All right. I'm probably doing something I'll regret." He stared at the boy, who continued to sob uncontrollably. "You got ten seconds to get up and get the hell out of here. And nine of them are gone."

The boy jumped up, ran to the door, opened it and ran out, slamming it behind him.

The man stared at the closed door for several seconds then replaced his revolver in his belt holster. He walked to the table and began replacing rods and patches and cloth back into the gun kit box.

Suddenly, from the inner hallway leading from the bathroom, a middle-aged man appeared. He was slim and dark and unhappy. And dripping wet. His clothes appeared to be covered with blood. He carried a pair of dry shoes over to the sofa and placed them on the floor.

"If I had to stay in that bathtub one more fucking minute I would be dead for real. As it is, I may have got pneumonia. I still say I coulda just been on the bed."

As he spoke, he grabbed the clean clothes and towel from the television set and stepped back into the hallway. He raised his voice while he changed. "What the hell did I have to be in the tub for, anyway?"

"I told you: it looks better."

"Yeah, right. It looks better."

"He might have checked you out on the bed. Nobody touches a body in a tub full of bloody water."

"That right? Well, you're the expert. But I got ketchup in my hair, my nose, my ears... my eyes, for fuck's sake!"

The big man said nothing. The man with ketchup in his hair quickly finished changing and walked back into the room. "First time I ever made money playing a corpse. How about you? You ever played a corpse?"

"Never did."

"You shoulda taken the punk's wallet. I'll bet he was loaded. He offered it to you, didn't he?"

"I'm not a thief."

"Well, pardon me all over the fuckin' place, but where I come from money is money." The slim man suddenly sneezed three times in a row. "See? I'm getting pneumonia from that tub. And it's not like I got health insurance or somethin'."

The big man finished packing up his gun kit. Folding the newspaper neatly, he dropped it into a trash can. He lowered himself slowly into a chair and waited for the slim man. He stared at the stylized painting of the village. It could be any Thai village. He'd left his after his first hit. And never returned. Images of long ago flickered across his mind. A beautiful young girl, a competing suitor, the flash of a knife, blood, screaming, running, hiding.

The slim man sneezed again before he could get his sentence out. "You got health insurance?"

"No. "

"I don't know anybody in the business who does. Who the hell can afford it on what Wichai pays? What pisses me off is that punk kid is gonna go to a college in the States and fuck lotsa blondes and drink lotsa beer and end up in business with his corrupt uncle and makin' a fortune. And me? I'm gonna croak from not having health insurance."

He rubbed his hair vigorously with the towel and then sat on the couch. He angrily put his socks and shoes on. "We didn't get enough."

"Forty thousand baht apiece to scare a kid out of the business? Seems pretty fair to me."

Yeah, forty thousand baht will pay off a few gambling debts. But how much did the kid's uncle pay Wichai to hire us? What's Wichai's take? You know who that kid is? Who his uncle is? I mean—"

"I don't care about Wichai's take. But…"

The slim man noticed the hesitation. "What?"

"I don't like it."

"What?"

"I'm good at what I do. I don't like this kind of thing. The money's not clean."

"Money's dirty to you unless you took somebody out for it?"

"It doesn't feel right. It feels phony. "

"What's phony about it?"

"I acted out what I am. I only pretended to do what I do. And took money for it. So what am I? A whore? I feel like a goddamn actor."

"*You?* An actor! That's a good one. Yeah, well, if it makes you unhappy, you can always give me your share. 'Cause the only thing don't feel right to me is havin' no money. How I get it is never the question."

The big man remained in his thoughtful mood. "I wish somebody had done that for me when I was his age."

"Done what?"

"Kept me out of the business."

"The slim man stared at him, shook his head and then continued checking himself in the mirror for any remaining traces of ketchup. "You! Man, you are in some mood today. That kid musta spooked you. I couldn't believe his bullshit about the Kaeochart hit. I thought you might take him out just for trying to take the credit."

"Kaeochart was a clean hit."

The slim man interrupted combing his hair to stare at the big man, finished combing it and then walked to the door and opened it. "I don't know about you, but I'm getting the hell out of here." He exited into the hallway and left the door open.

The big man listened to the sound of the slim man's receding footsteps. He glanced again at the painting and then pushed his large frame up and out of the chair. He picked up his gun case, walked to the door and paused in the doorway to look back into the room. He spoke aloud but to no one. "I just wish somebody had done that for me."

He exited the room and closed the door behind him.

Dean Barrett

Dean Barrett is the author of several novels set in Asia - *Memoirs of a Bangkok Warrior, Hangman's Point* (Hong Kong); *Kingdom of Make-Believe* (Thailand); *Skytrain to Murder* (Thailand); *Identity Theft* (Thailand and Florida), *Mistress of the East* (1862 China).

His recent books are *Murder at the Horny Toad Bar & other Outrageous Tales of Thailand* and *The Go Go Dancer Who Stole My Viagra and Other Poetic Tragedies of Thailand. Dragon Slayer* is a book with three novellas on Chinese themes. His latest, *Permanent Damage*, is a sequel to *Skytrain to Murder*, a detective novel set in Thailand starring Scott Sterling.

Barrett's plays have been performed in nine countries and his musical, *Fragrant Harbour*, set in 1857 Hong Kong, was selected by the National Alliance for Musical Theater to be staged on 42nd Street.

The Sword

Vasit Dejkunjorn

From the glass window Yuddha could see the blue
BMW Series 5, parked in the roofed parking lot in
front of his office. Yuddha was aware of his colleagues' concealed suspicion. But he ignored it. After
all, he was not the only police superintendent—full
colonel—who owned an expensive European-made
car. Another superintendent, his classmate from the
Police Officer Academy, had bought a Mercedes. Yet
another colonel owned a Lexus, Japanese-made but
equally priced. To own and drive an expensive car is
a dream of every police officer. Yuddha guessed that
the other cars had been obtained by means not much
different from his.

It had begun soon after his graduation from the
Academy. He had been assigned to a police station
in Bangkok. His responsibility was to interrogate
suspects brought in by arresting officers and to
submit interrogation reports to the superintendent,
with recommendations that the suspects be charged
or else released for insufficient evidence.

Yuddha learned quickly that his recommendation might change the suspect's fate. With a few clicks of his notebook mouse, the suspect might be freed— or start his rough journey to the penitentiary. He learned too that every suspect was willing to pay for his freedom. Yuddha was no longer surprised when approached by some of his superiors who suggested, often with straight faces, that he fact-twist for the benefit of the superiors' relatives or friends. At first he felt awkward and ashamed, but finally he gave in and jumped on the bandwagon.

Yuddha's popularity-cum-notoriety grew steadily, proportionate to his wealth. He was recognized by superior officers, envied by colleagues and quietly feared by both the innocent and the crooks. To superior officers, Yuddha was always generous. He managed to appear, though uninvited, with appropriate, expensive gifts at police generals' birthdays, New Year parties or wedding anniversaries. If there was a donation involved, his amount was always among the highest.

So when Yuddha's name was submitted to the selection board, with long, elaborate, praising explanation by his commissioner, none of the board members objected or questioned the submission. At forty-two Yuddha became one the youngest police colonels and superintendents on the force. In the seniority list there had been over 100 names above his.

Yuddha progressed with his lucrative police work. He did not forget that criminal investigation and interrogation alone were not sufficient for his fame. To be hailed as a police idol, he would have to show that he was skilled too in crime suppression. The young superintendent consequently turned to the easiest prey: the petty thieves. His arrest records were impressively long. When an armed robber resisted arrest, Yuddha did not waste time negotiating. The robber was gunned down in a brief firefight. With the extrajudicial killing, Yuddha joined the prestigious class of police exterminators.

Yuddha's trail of thought was interrupted by a middle-aged warrant officer's entry. The non-commissioned officer did not stop to salute him but casually sat himself on a chair and said unceremoniously, "Sia Preeda has returned and wants to see you." The article "Sia" is a Chinese word, indicating the man's origin and his status in business. Yuddha had been expecting the return of the Sia. He nodded his head in acknowledgement. The warrant officer too knew the reason for the superintendent's expectation. Expressionlessly, he rose and left the room.

While waiting, Yuddha recalled the incident that had led to the confrontation between him and Sia Preeda. The businessman had been involved in a car accident that resulted in the death of a motorcyclist. Such accidents are routine in Bangkok and no longer reported by the media. According to the crime scene investigator, the speeding motorcycle had crashed into Sia Preeda's Mercedes. The businessman's expensive car was heavily dented. The fault was obviously the dead motorcyclist's. But technically, according to the Criminal Code, the driver of the Mercedes was to be arrested and charged for careless driving causing death.

Sia Preeda had accompanied his driver to the police station and requested bail for the unfortunate chauffeur. It was Friday afternoon. Unless the bail was quickly granted, the driver might have to spend the weekend in the police detention cell. The superintendent has the power to approve or deny bail. In this case the investigating officer had recommended that bail be granted.

For experienced but dishonest police officers, this was an ideal opportunity to make easy money. Yuddha flipped the pages of the investigator's report, feigning reading. A few pages afterward, he looked up and told the businessman, "Looks like your driver was going a little fast."

"Fast?" Sia Preeda and his driver were obviously shocked. "We were approaching a very busy inter-section. The traffic was—"

"I am aware of the traffic condition." The superintendent's voice was raised and ice-cold. "It was congested, yes, but you were going beyond the speed limit, as the skid marks show. Incidentally, who was actually driving the car at the time of the accident?"

"Who?" Sia Preeda repeated the word in disbelief. "What do you mean, who?"

"I was driving, sir," the driver offered meekly.

"That remains to be seen," the Colonel's voice was offish. "In the meantime I am afraid we may have to hold both of you for additional questioning."

"This is ridiculous!" the businessman nearly screamed. "I am going to call my lawyer."

"After you have been charged," the superintendent said in a toneless voice, "you may call anyone you like. But we have to seize your phone too. It's an important piece of evidence."

While Sia Preeda was speechlessly trying to control his temper, the young colonel pushed a button on his desk. The warrant officer entered the room, approached the desk and waited for the stern order.

"Book these two men as suspects in the accident case."

The warrant officer knew exactly what he should do. He had done it many times before. Once outside, he told the businessman: "Sia, there is a way this can be settled without any complexity. You and your driver don't have to be locked up, spend the night in the cell and go to court tomorrow." The officer's voice was soft and soothing. Sia Preeda lowered the hand holding the mobile phone. The warrant officer did not wait for a response but proceeded with his advice: "The superintendent is a contestant in the annual departmental programme for police station development. But he is short of funds. With some voluntary donations, the station can be renovated, the lawn mowed, the flagstaff repainted. Besides, donation means public support. The superintendent will earn additional points in the contest and have a better chance of winning."

"Wh-what about the accident case?" The businessman was not convinced.

"Take my word. All you have to do is go back to the superintendent and offer a sum—er, donation— and everything will be all right. You will be freed, although your driver will have to be charged. But the investigating officer will conclude it was the fault of the dead motorcyclist. He will recommend that the driver be released on bail, and the charge will be dropped. Believe me, it's routine."

"But there's still the prosecutor." Sia Preeda showed he knew some legal procedures. "He may disagree with the investigating officer. And what about the motorcyclist's family?"

"The prosecutor will agree." The warrant officer's raised voice indicated he was annoyed. "As for your Mercedes, it is insured, right? First-class? Will the insurance company not handle the matter for you?"

"How much should I offer for the... er, dona- tion?" Sia Preecha asked the expected question.

He was shocked when given the amount. "Fifty thousand baht! I think I'll call my lawyer."

"Go ahead." The warrant officer's soft and soothing tone was gone. "I'll take you to the investigating officer. He will charge the driver and charge you as an accomplice in the accident case. You and your driver will be detained and denied bail. I don't know what the lawyer's fee is, but in a case like yours I presume it won't be low."

The warrant officer waited while Sia Preecha was pondering an alternative. He was certain of the businessman's next sentence. And he was right, as always.

"Okay, but I don't have enough cash. I'll have to write a cheque."

"No cheque." It was an order. "The superintendent does not accept cheques, only cash. There are two ATMs in front of the station, next door to the 7-Eleven."

Five minutes later, Sia Preeda was back in the superintendent's cozy office. He found the Colonel sitting comfortably on the padded leather chair, intensely watching an ongoing football match between two famous British teams.

"I... I understand, sir, that you are in the process of developing this police station to win a contest," Sia Preeda's wavering voice reflected his total submission. "I would like to help by making a—er, donation."

The superintendent turned around in his swiveling chair, smilingly facing the businessman, and responded in a friendly tone. "I appreciate your kind interest in the police business. As you must have already known, the police serve the public. But our budgetary capability is very limited. So public support like yours is always welcomed. We will never forget your kindness."

Half an hour later, Sia Preeda found himself out of the police station in his Mercedes with the bailed driver. Leaving the premises, he spotted the shining blue BMW parked in the roofed garage under a sign that read "Superintendent." The businessman could now guess where his donation would be going.

The young police colonel eyed the white envelope he had just accepted from Sia Preeda. Yuddha knew that, according to the Criminal Code, he had just made another offence of willfully accepting a bribe. If caught and proven guilty, he might be sentenced to serve years in a state penitentiary. But the superintendent was not worried. Sia Preeda was a wealthy businessman. In his business his profit must be huge, incomparable to the Colonel's meagre salaries. It was a fair game in which no one was hurt. Yuddha believed he deserved the 50,000 baht he had just squeezed from Sia Preeda.

He opened the envelope and took 5,000 from the stack. As a usual practice, the amount would go to the warrant officer—his broker—for another service rendered.

Yuddha opened his Samsonite briefcase and threw in the envelope. The 45,000 baht would join the millions in the safe at his house. He never trusted the bank, although he maintained a modest account there, in case someone investigated.

The warrant officer entered the office without knocking, pocketed his earnings, deposited some mail on the desk and left. Yuddha looked at his watch and saw that it was close to six o'clock in the evening—time for dinner. His dinner date was a young, extremely attractive and extremely rich lady. Yuddha had been steadily courting the girl for a year and seriously planning to marry her. The wealthy girl, though openly affectionate, had been evading his engagement proposals. Yuddha did not want to miss the dinner or keep her waiting.

He rose, but a posted envelope on the desk caught his attention. The crude handwriting on the envelope looked familiar. Then Yuddha saw the name of the sender and the return address and recognized them. Slowly he sat down, opened the envelope and read the short, simple letter.

"My dearest son Yuddha,

"I have bad news. The doctor has just told me that I have a final stage cancer and don't have long to live. As you know, you are my most beloved son. So after I die, I want you to handle all of my money and property, to make sure that you, your brother and your sister have fair shares. As you already know, as a farmer, I do not have much, but I hope what I give you will help you some. Please come to see me as soon as you can—before it is too late.

"Your loving father,

"Samarn"

Yuddha felt as though he had been hit on the head with a mallet. He could not move. The superintendent stared at the letter and had a strange feeling that it was staring back at him, accusingly. Samarn was not his father. The superintendent's parents had died in a road accident years before he finished high school. He had since been under the care of a poor uncle who lived from hand to mouth, with many mouths to feed, including Yuddha's. The Police Officer Academy, for Yuddha, had been god-sent, as every cadet was given official status and pay that helped relieve his financial burden.

It was when Yuddha was in his second year at the Academy that he was sent, under a programme, to live like a stepson with a family in a rural province. The programme was designed for the cadet to familiarize himself with the rustic farmer's life, and to demolish the traditional barrier that separates the police from the public. It was hoped that the experience would be imprinted on the cadet's mind and memory so that, after his graduation and at the beginning of his police career, he would recall the hardship of his stepfamily and be understanding and sympathetic when serving the public.

Samarn's family had been selected for Cadet Yuddha. The week of home stay had resulted in a strong bond between Yuddha the stepson and Samarn the stepfather and his family. Before Yuddha left the family to return to the Academy, Samarn gave his police stepson a bag of straw mushrooms as a going-away present. "Son," Samarn had said, "you won't be able to live on the low police pay. Grow the mushrooms and sell them. It will supplement your pay and enable you to maintain your integrity and be a good policeman."

Samarn and his family were invited to witness the graduation ceremony. The man wept when he saw Yuddha kneeling down in front of the King, who presented Yuddha with a sword. The sword is symbolic but significant, as it marks the beginning of the long, hard road of police life.

After the graduation the bond between Yuddha and his stepfamily weakened and diminished. The ceremonial sword was kept in its scabbard, occasionally used together with white gloves when required.

Yuddha nearly jumped when his thoughts were rudely interrupted by the piercing sound of his cellular phone. It was the girl. The superintendent mumbled a weak excuse, telling his date he was tied up by an urgent, unexpected errand and would be with her shortly.

The young colonel was reaching for his briefcase when he was interrupted again by a voice. It was his very own voice. The words were familiar. It was a pledge uttered by all cadets in the Temple of the Emerald Buddha, following their admittance to the Academy. The voice came in loud and clear:

"I pledge to perform my duty with utmost integrity and honesty, to devote myself in serving the people, and to be a police officer with full moral and ethical principles;

"I pledge to enforce the law altruistically and justly, and not to be influenced by personal feeling, aversion, bias or gratuity in making my decision;

"If I violate this pledge, may my life be plagued by misery, despair, misfortune and disaster: may my life end with extreme pain and in torment;

"If I remain true to this pledge, may I be blessed with mental and physical strength, ability to overcome obstacles and evil; may I be blessed with happiness, advancement and continued success in my official and private life."

The words of the pledge still echoing in his ears, Yuddha turned toward the altar in his office. On it were Buddha's images of various sizes, most of which had been purchased by him or given by well-wishers. Just below the altar stood his graduation sword in its gleaming scabbard. Absent-mindedly, the young colonel approached the altar and the sword. He grabbed the sword and gently pulled it out of the

250

scabbard. Yuddha saw that the engraved blade was still shining despite the years that had passed. His thoughts returned to the graduation day: the moment before his name had been announced by the Commissioner of the Academy, the steps he had cautiously taken toward His Majesty the King and the sword he had accepted directly from the King's hands.

The phone rang again. This time Yuddha did not hear it. The only thing he heard was the pledge he had solemnly made in the Temple of the Emerald Buddha.

At 20:00 hours, the duty officer knocked on the door of the superintendent's office. He had not seen the superintendent leave and presumed the superior officer was still in the office. He knocked again. When there was no response, the officer decided to pull the door open and stepped inside.

The lifeless body of the superintendent was found lying face up on the carpeted floor. His eyes were wide open. The pool of blood under and around the body looked fresh. At the left side of Yuddha's chest, about two thirds of the sword blade was visible. The rest was embedded in his chest. The grip was swaying a little, as though it had just been left there by somebody.

"Looks like suicide," remarked the lieutenant colonel who headed the crime scene investigation team, after preliminary examination. "No sign of foul play."

Later in the night, the medical examiner reported to the Metropolitan Police Commissioner a puzzling, disturbing finding: the sword bore no fingerprint, not even a smudge. It looked brand new, untouched and unused, ever.

Pol. Gen. Vasit Dejkunjorn

Police General Vasit Dejkunjorn has had a long and distinguished career as a police officer, newspaper columnist and writer. Widely regarded as a public servant with high integrity and professionalism, as a career police officer he served as police inspector-general, deputy director-general of the Royal Thai Police, chief of Royal Court Police, and after his retirement, senator and deputy minister of interior. He started his career in literature early. Since his time as a student at Chulalongkorn University in the late 1940s, he has written thousands of articles, numerous short stories and over 20 novels. His Thai-language novels have been best-sellers among Thai readers and made into films and TV series such as *Hak Lin Chang* (หักลิ้นช้าง), *Sarawat Yai* (สารวัตรใหญ่), and many more. He was named National Artist in Literature in 1998.

Now in his retirement, Pol. Gen. Vasit continues his writing as well as his public service work in various capacities, including as special court police officer and vice president of Transparency Thailand. He also lectures on management and ethics and teaches Buddhist meditation.

The Lunch That Got Away

Eric Stone

"Sorry, no fish today, Khun Ray." Plaa looks more upset by that than she ought to be.

Maybe she has sold out. I hope so, for her sake. But it is still early, and this would be the first time ever.

"Plaa, is something wrong?"

"No, no problem, Khun Ray, only no fish today."

She's a bad liar.

"Come on, what is it?" She bites her lip and looks away. I can barely hear her.

"Robbers, Khun Ray, take fish and all my money. Make big trouble for me."

I've been buying lunch from Plaa for a few years. She makes the absolute best green curry-coated, banana leaf-wrapped baked fish I've ever had. And she sells it every day out of her cooler on the street at

Sukhumvit Soi 11, across from my hotel, for twenty-five baht.

I'm in town for one hellish day of appointments. Our Bangkok correspondent is mad at the editor of the magazine. I can't blame him. I am, too. But I don't see why he had to take it out on me. I guess it's my fault for letting him arrange my schedule.

My first appointment was an interview at the Central Bank at four-thirty this morning. The guy I met gets into the office at three to avoid traffic. My last interview is set for seven this evening, back next door to the Central Bank. In between I've got four more appointments scattered all over town. Those six interviews are going to add up to a total of about three hours of work, for which I'm going to spend at least twelve hours stuck in traffic.

I like Bangkok when I don't need to get anywhere.

At least the correspondent has loaned me his rolling office, so I can work at the desk in the back of the van as his brother-in-law drives me around town. And, having been the one who introduced me to Plaa's fish, he didn't want her to lose out on my business, so he has kindly routed us past her usual spot just before lunch.

"When did this happen, Plaa?"

"I get here ten o'clock, Khun Ray. They waiting for me, push me, take cooler, run away."

That was an hour ago, and Bangkok is a very big city. I doubt there's much I can do.

But I like Plaa. She works hard and spends little on herself so she can afford to keep her fifteen-year-old daughter Noi in school and out of the bars. I'm here to write an economic update on the country. My appointments are all with big shots. But it's Plaa and people like her that actually make this place tick.

"Do you know who it was? Did you recognize them?"

In Bangkok everybody knows who everybody else is, at least within their neighborhoods. And why would anyone come across town to rob a street vendor?

She gets a look on her face that I don't like. A look that tells me she knows who it was but doesn't want to say.

I ask again and she pretends she doesn't understand me. I know she does. Her English isn't good, but it's good enough.

There's a tap on my shoulder. It's Cho, my driver for the day. He wants to get me back in the van. We've only got an hour to get to the next appointment, and it's a couple of miles away. I'd walk if it wasn't ninety-nine degrees and ninety–some-odd percent humidity and not likely to rain at any minute, and I'm not in a suit.

Cho wants to be a journalist. I have him sit in on my interviews in case I need any translation. It's a matter of pride for him that we're punctual, no matter how bad the traffic.

But I don't want to let this drop. I'm getting tired of hearing all the glowing reports about the booming Thai economy. I could already write exactly what the next three interviews are going to tell me. "It's 1992. If the economy keeps growing at eleven percent a year, by 2000 it will be blah blah blah." I can do the optimistic math as well as the next well-connected mogul or government minister. It all sounds too good to be true, which it is.

Plaa's got a real problem, maybe one I can do something about.

"Cho, Plaa was robbed. I think she knows who did it, but she won't tell me. Could you ask her?"

He leads her a few feet away, their backs turned. They talk for a minute before Cho comes back to tell me what he's found out. Plaa stays where she is but turns toward us. Her face is pointed down, but I can see she's looking at us through the tops of her eyes.

"I think maybe better we go to your appointment, Khun Ray. This maybe big trouble. Better we not involved."

"What's the problem?"

"Man who steal from Plaa work for Big Shrimp."

The name sounds familiar. "What's that?"

"Big new restaurant, Sukhumvit 37. Owned by wife of general."

I'd heard of it. There was a small stink raised when an old apartment building full of working-class people was torn down to clear the land for it. And the general himself has recently been associated with some shady land deals. But wives of generals are well-connected.

"Huh? What would they want with Plaa's fish? And she couldn't have had much money."

"They want know how Plaa cook her fish. They offer her money, but she not want to tell. Her cook same as mother and grandmother. Is family secret. Today they steal fish and money and tell Plaa if she not tell, then she no do business any more."

It takes some persuasion. At first she doesn't want help from a *farang*, but we get Plaa into the van. I call and cancel my next appointment as we make our way in fits and starts the twenty-six blocks to Big Shrimp.

It's not the world's biggest restaurant. That's another twenty or so blocks farther down Sukhumvit. Big Shrimp is too classy for cute waitresses on roller skates, but not by much. It's over-decorated in the sort of Mekong whisky-fueled, faux Edwardian *trompe-l'oeil* taste that infected elements of the Thai upper classes in the 1970s. The illuminated walls and ceiling are lousy with 3-D wood nymphs and angels and fat cherubs. There's a long entryway lined with alcoves, painted to look like aquariums stocked with comely mermaids and muscular mermen. There's not a molding, frame or edge of anything I can see that isn't painted gold. I've heard the food's pretty good, but the place doesn't do much for my appetite.

Neither does the big man at the door to the office. He's taller than me, really tall for a Thai guy. He's heavy and thick with muscle, not fat. He's got scars on his face, and his nose has been broken enough that I know he's not averse to a scrape. Maybe the scariest thing about him is his suit. It's shiny black, rich, dense wool, two buttons buttoned. The hallway's not air-conditioned, and he isn't sweating.

I am, but I'm always sweating in Bangkok. I can talk to him all day, too, but it soon becomes plain he isn't going to react to a thing I have to say.

Cho steps up to translate, but the big fella doesn't react to him either. I'm tempted to snap my fingers in front of his face, but I'm afraid he could snap me in two if I were to irritate him. So I don't.

I step back and whisper to Plaa, who is keeping her distance.

"Is he one of the guys who robbed you?"

She shakes her head no. That makes sense. There's no point in wasting a heavy like this on lightweight street work. There are plenty of ambitious teenagers around who a rich woman can find for that sort of thing.

But we're not going to get anywhere even if we find who actually did it. To fix this thing, we need to talk with the boss. And she's through the door on the other side of the thug.

She knows we're here. There's a security camera above the door, covering the hallway.

I step in front of it, thinking I'll talk to the camera since I'm not getting anything out of the big guy. But he's quick. He moves in front of me, blocking me from view.

Maybe there's sound. I try talking, but the guy smiles at me in a way that I think means I'm talking to myself. We need to figure out another approach.

We start walking away. Out on the street in front, I suggest to Plaa and Cho that we go somewhere. I'll buy lunch, and we can talk over what to do next.

Plaa's face lights up. I think she's happy I'm going to buy lunch, but I'm wrong. She leans into Cho's ear and whispers to him. His face lights up, too, and they both turn to me, smiling.

"Khun Ray, Plaa has a good idea." I turn to her and she starts explaining in rapid-fire Thai, gesturing at the Big Fish restaurant.

Cho also points at the restaurant. "We go back in here, sit down, okay?"

No, I don't think that's okay. I don't want to give Big Fish my money. I give the two of them a look.

"No problem, Khun Ray. You do not understand." Cho leans in to explain the plan to me. It's a good one, and as we walk back inside, I hand Plaa my mobile phone. Cho's already making calls on his.

The lunch crowd hasn't come in yet, and we have our choice of tables. We sit down in the middle of the restaurant at a table that could comfortably seat six people. I order one large Kloster beer for Cho and me to split. Plaa wants hot tea.

The two of them are making calls on the mobile phones while I leaf through the menu. It actually does look pretty good, and I'm hungry. But that's not the plan.

The waiter comes up to take our order, and we send him away, saying we're going to wait for our friends to get here. Plaa hands me back my phone, and I make a few calls of my own.

I'm thirsty, so I lift my glass and take a small sip of my beer. Cho wags a finger at me, and I put the glass back down. He hasn't touched his, and Plaa is letting her tea get cold.

We've been putting off the waiter for almost a half hour when the lunch crowd begin to arrive, taking their places in twos and threes at tables for four or more. I notice Plaa and Cho making very slight nods, little waves of no more than a finger at the people who are coming into the restaurant.

These aren't the typical, well-heeled patrons of the place. The customers have dressed as nice as they can for the occasion, but their best is a lot lower on the fashion scale than Big Shrimp's usual lunch crowd of businessmen. The restaurant staff are giving each other looks, wondering, "Who are these people? Can they afford to eat here?"

Our Bangkok correspondent comes in. He's with the Thai editor of a local trouble-making magazine and his chief reporter, a tiny but solid-looking Thai woman from the country's dirt-poor northeast. She's known for her motto, a quote from an American journalist of the early 1900s: "To afflict the comfortable, and comfort the afflicted." I flash them a smile. They sit down at a table in a corner from where they can observe the whole restaurant.

By the time the restaurant's full, there are only two tables that appear to actually be ordering lunch. Everyone else has no more than one cooling or warming drink in front of them and can't make up their mind about what they want to eat. The waiters, maitre d' and floor managers are in a huddle by the motionless swinging doors to the kitchen. Every so often a busboy or cook's face appears in one of the windows in the kitchen doors, grins broadly and then disappears.

A crowd of the usual customers gathers at the front desk, wanting their usual tables. They're increasingly restless, perturbed in their fine summer-weight wools and linens. But too bad. Big Shrimp is full.

The maitre d' hurries over to try and mollify his customers, but most of them turn and walk away. There are plenty of other places to eat nearby. A few agree to take empty seats at some of the partially filled tables.

A man in one of the most perfectly tailored suits I've ever seen with a haircut that no doubt cost as much as Plaa makes in a month or more sits down at our table. He's with a Miss Universe-class, bejewelled woman of about a third his age. They smile at me and look nervously at my lunch companions.

Cho says something to the beautiful woman that brings out a big smile on Plaa's face. The woman looks startled and turns to the man, who looks annoyed.

He turns to me and in impeccable, upper-class British English, with just the barest tint of a Thai accent, asks what it is that I "make of all this"? It hasn't occurred to him that I'm part of it.

I explain what's going on, and as I do I can see the turmoil going on inside him. Despite his best efforts, it's emblazoned across his face. The part of him that has spent a lot of time outside Thailand wants to argue with me. But he is Thai, after all, and arguing is either beneath him or just not done.

At first it looks like he might ignore us, order lunch and go about his business. But when the woman tugs on his arm and whispers to him, he gets up, shooting me something uncertain between a smile and a grimace, and they walk out.

Most of the other people who had sat down at already occupied tables get up to leave as well. The maitre d' tries stopping them at the door, but no one's listening to him. Finally he gives up and retreats down the hallway toward the office guarded by the big man.

The waiters aren't even bothering to come around anymore. They know no one's going to order anything. Once in a while someone will take a very small sip of the drink in front of them, but that's all any of us are having for lunch.

The big guy and the maitre d' come back out of the hallway and look the place over. The big guy says something to him, and their eyes focus on our table. The maitre d' gestures for one of the head waiters to come over and has him take his place by the door as the muscle and he go outside.

The maitre d' is back in about ten minutes with an impressive looking cop. He's in a crisp, ironed uniform with polished gold buttons and military insignia. They head down the hallway to the office.

The restaurant is silent. No one is talking at their tables. The staff look on with their mouths firmly shut. There's no clatter from the kitchen.

In short order the cop, the bruiser and the maitre d' stream out of the hallway and make a beeline for our table. I stand up, preparing to take the brunt of whatever it is they've decided to do with us.

Something moves in the far periphery of my vision. I look over, and it's the Thai magazine editor and his bulldog reporter getting up from their table and also making quickly toward ours. This is going to be interesting.

Both groups reach us at the same time. Maybe the small cassette recorder in the outstretched arm of the reporter beats out the maitre d' by a hair. They all stop and look at each other.

The reporter and editor look expectant, enthusiastic. This could be exactly the sort of story that their readers really eat up.

The maitre d' looks like he's about to start stomping his feet and spitting. The heavy looks like he just wants to stomp somebody, anybody, bad.

The cop looks nervous. He's supposed to be there on the side of Big Shrimp, but he's got higher-ups to answer to and they don't like publicity. He throws me a look, like maybe I can help him out of this jam.

Plaa and Cho are sitting quietly. They've moved their drinks in a little closer and bent their heads over them. Their eyes flick up and back down to look at the six of us standing around the table. Everyone else in the restaurant is looking, too, and not being discreet about it.

There's a flash of light and then another. We all look around, and there's the correspondent of my magazine with a camera. I turn back to face the maitre d' and his posse and paste a big grin on my face.

"Smile, fellas."

The big guy starts moving in the direction of my correspondent, but he's by the front door and scurries out. He gives up, steps back and makes a move to snatch the tape recorder from the reporter, but the maitre d' puts out a hand to stop him.

No one's got guns out, but it's beginning to feel like a Mexican standoff.

The maitre d' steps around the table up to me and speaks low so that no one else can hear.

"You want order lunch now, mister?" Despite the words, it isn't really a question.

"We might after a while. My friends and I are thirsty. We want to enjoy our drinks first." I don't shout, but I make sure I'm loud enough to be heard by the people at nearby tables.

He looks down at Plaa and Cho and then around the whole dining room. He looks back at me with an unhappy smile. He wishes I could help him out, too. It was a mistake speaking to me. If it had been Cho or Plaa, or most of the other Thai people in the restaurant, he could simply have insisted that they leave.

The maitre d' turns and talks to the cop. I think he's asking if there's anything he can do.

But the cop wants no part of it. He raises his hands in what appears to be some form of surrender, smiles, shrugs his shoulders, turns on his heels and walks out as quickly as he can without looking like he's running.

The big guy's had enough. He starts toward me, his hands out. Taking apart a *farang* in front of a whole restaurant and a muckraking reporter and editor is not a smart move. But I don't think he's really thought it out. He's just itching to do something to earn his keep.

The maitre d' looks horrified. He knows this is not good. But he's not about to get between me and anybody's fists or feet.

It's fight or flight. I don't have much time to make up my mind.

The pager on the bruiser's belt makes it up for me. It buzzes, freezing him in his tracks. He takes a look at the display and unclips it to show the maitre d', and the both of them head back to the office pronto.

I sit back down, wishing I could gulp my beer even if it is warm and flat. Instead, I take a small, awful sip.

In about a minute the maitre d' has returned by himself. He leans down to whisper in my ear.

"Khunying Preeya ask to have the pleasure of your company in the office."

It seems unlikely that she'd have the big guy work me over anywhere on the premises, but I'm not sure.

"Please thank Khunying Preeya for me, but I am enjoying the company of my friends and the hospitality of her restaurant. If she would like to come to our table, I will be happy to buy her a drink and make her welcome."

Once again he looks like he doesn't know what to do. I almost feel bad for him as he quick-steps back to the office.

The reporter and editor are still standing by the table, and I gesture to them to sit down. The reporter puts her cassette recorder down between us. I cover it with a hand.

"I'm not the one you want to interview."

"Yeah, but the interview I'm after won't talk to me." She's been to school in the U.S. I can hear it in her voice.

"Who's that?"

"Who do you think? The General, Khunying's husband. He's the real story in this place."

I'm sure he is. There've been rumors swirling around him for weeks, but there's no way she's going to get to him.

"Okay, but what's going on at the moment is about my friend here, Khun Plaa. It's her you should be talking to." I explain the situation.

From the look on her face, I can almost see the wheels and cogs begin to spin in her brain. She smiles at me, gets up and moves to sit next to Plaa. They bend their heads together to talk.

The editor looks at me and smiles. Then he says something to Cho, who translates. The editor's apologized for not speaking English. I apologize in return for not speaking Thai. He and Cho bend their heads together in conversation.

It's getting late enough that I'll probably have to cancel my next appointment as well. I'm willing to do that, but I'm not sure how long I can sit here taking the occasional small sip of a beer gone bad.

My notebook sits in front of me like an accusation. I'd got it out thinking I'd at least make some notes about something, anything that I could write an article on for the magazine. My editor makes me crazy, but I don't want to give him any cause to fire me. How can I relate what's going on here now to the Thai economy, which is, after all, what I'm supposed to be covering?

I haven't got anywhere with that train of thought when the maitre d' reappears with the boss lady herself. The big guy stands back at the entrance to the office hall. I get up as they approach the table. She holds out a surprisingly indelicate, rough hand with three of its fingers bulging on either side of garish, expensive rings. She's wearing a severe gray silk suit, and her hair is done up in a coif I associate more with Texas than Thailand. She does not look happy.

"I am Khunying Preeya, and you are… ?"

"Ray Sharp."

"Why do you disturb my restaurant's lunch business, Mister Sharp?"

I invite her to sit down at the table, but she ignores me. I guess she left the standard social graces in her office.

"I have eaten, Mister Sharp. You and your associates have not. I insist that you order meals or that you leave the premises. This is a restaurant, Mister Sharp. It is not a waiting room."

"I am here, Khunying Preeya, to help my friend, Khun Plaa, recover the money and cooler that were stolen from her."

The boss lady looks down at Plaa and flutters a hand at her, then me. "Why are the troubles of a common street vendor of any concern to me?"

I smile and gesture to the restaurant around us. "Apparently they are, or will be."

"Are you threatening me, Mister Sharp? Do you know who my husband is? I am going to call him." She lifts a hand with a mobile phone in it.

Everyone knows who her husband is. He's politically connected, but word on the street lately is that some of his ties might be coming loose. There are more than slight whiffs of scandal. But he hasn't been talking. Generals who stay out of the public eye tend to last longer than those who don't. He won't want publicity.

"Go ahead. Maybe he will want to get mixed up in this. But I'd be surprised. For now, my friends like it here, Khunying Preeya. It is cool and comfortable. They could become regulars. I have a lot of friends, and my friends have friends as well."

"What do you want, Mister Sharp?"

"It's not about what I want." I almost say "lady," but you never get anywhere in Thailand by not at least pretending to be polite. "If you would be so kind as to speak with my friend Khun Plaa, I am sure you can work something out."

"She can come to my office." The boss lady begins to turn and walk away, and it takes a lot of effort for me to sound civil. If Plaa goes back there alone, who knows what might happen?

"I don't think my friend will feel comfortable in your office. This is such a nice room, and there is an empty table in the corner where you can have some privacy. It would be best if you spoke out here."

She almost loses her cool but keeps herself in check with no more than a minor harrumph. She crooks one of her heavily weighted fingers at Plaa and walks to the table that my correspondent, the editor and the reporter have left.

Plaa looks up at me, not sure what to do.

"Go, talk to her. Tell her what you want. You've got the power here."

She turns to the reporter, and they whisper to each other.

They get up together and follow the boss lady to the table. Plaa sits next to the *khunying*, the reporter across the table but still close enough to lend support.

Everyone in the restaurant is trying to look like they aren't trying to listen. There's no way to hear anything, but it's hard to be patient, especially when I'm so thirsty. I take a bigger sip and then a gulp of the terrible beer. There's still half of it left when I put it down, and it hasn't helped at all. It was just reminiscent enough of something refreshing to make my thirst worse.

After about five minutes the boss lady makes a call on her mobile phone. She says something, listens and then responds with something shrill, not quite a shriek, but close. She listens again and hands the phone to the reporter.

The reporter speaks briefly and then spends the next few minutes listening, taking notes and not saying anything. When she's done, she hands the phone back to the *khunying*, who begins talking but then stops in what is obviously mid-sentence. When she hangs up, she looks around the room frowning. She looks at Plaa and her body sags a little in her chair.

The boss lady gestures to the hallway. The big guy comes out and bends down to her. She whispers something and he hurries away. She stands up and says something that makes Plaa smile and the reporter shrug her shoulders. Then she walks away toward her office.

The two of them return to our table. Plaa sits down, still smiling, and takes a big sip of her now cool tea. The reporter leans in to whisper to her editor. He smiles, then frowns, then smiles again.

She sees me watching them, and when she's done talking to the editor, she looks at me.

"I talked with the General."

"Get anything interesting?"

"No, just a statement, but it means your friend Khun Plaa gets her cooler back and they'll leave her alone in the future."

"Great, but what's in it for you?"

"We'll be the only paper that's got anything at all from the General."

"Sure, but it's just him blowing his own horn."

"It's a start."

"How?"

"It raises his profile. That's not good for a general in this country."

"Give him enough rope?"

"Hopefully."

About ten minutes later the big guy walks up to the table looking like he's about to explode. I begin to get up, not sure what I can do. But all he does is roughly drop Plaa's cooler onto the table in front of her. The sound booms across the quiet restaurant.

Plaa stands up to look into her cooler. When she closes the lid again, she's smiling.

The editor waves a waiter over and orders drinks, cold and hot ones, whatever anybody wants, for the whole restaurant.

Cho and I share a tall, frosty Kloster before heading out to the van and back into the traffic. I might even make it to my last two appointments.

I still didn't get my fish for lunch. Next time.

Eric Stone

Eric Stone has worked as a writer, photographer, editor, publisher and publishing consultant. As a writer he's covered a wide range of topics, including business, economics, finance, politics, arts, culture, sports, and travel. For eleven years he lived in Asia, based in Hong Kong, then Jakarta. He's best known for his Ray Sharp PI series, set in Asia and based on stories he covered as a journalist, including *Shanghaied*, *Flight of the Hornbill*, *Grave Imports*, and *Living Room of the Dead*. He currently lives in Los Angeles.

Hot Enough to Kill

Collin Piprell

The sun burns a white-hot hole in the sky over Bangkok. Eyes are filled with disquiet; street dogs slink, panting, from shade to shade. According to the radio, this is the hottest April in fifty years.

Sombat the legless boy down the road was found dead yesterday, still upright on his little wooden cart, the one he propelled by hauling back on the steel crane-operator's lever. It was amazing how, so frail, he clattered and squeaked around the neighborhood, honed down to sinew and spirit, yanking away on that big handle. But yesterday was too hot, and he tried to go too far too fast. Or maybe he just got tired of it all. Who knows? He sat there as though asleep, breathless, like the day itself, motionless as the leaves on the trees behind the temple wall, his face drawn but peaceful.

The lane where Chai stays with his brother Vajira and his brother's wife is all but deserted. Vajira is surprised that Chai isn't going to the temple. Everybody liked the boy, and there's to be a *tamboon*, a merit-making ceremony, to mark his passing. But Chai has something he must do today. It's too hot to move, really, but this is something he has to do. It's going to bring in money. Good money. And his brother Vajira has been paying for everything the past couple of months. The temple is all very well. It's a good thing. But right now money comes first. There will be time for the temple later. So he has come to meet his new partner, into the middle of the city in the traffic and the heat, to do this job.

And now he's waiting.

A little way along, on the other side of the pedestrian overpass from where Chai waits, a beggar sits at his station. He's older than Sombat was, but just as legless, the legs of his short pants pinned up and empty. His face is full of mortification, his life one long humiliation. As people come by, he rattles the few coins in his cup, supplicant, bending forward to bang forehead and cup on the steel deck, piss-pools either side of his head. A legless beggar in a puddle of his own urine, left by his handlers for a long day shift on the overpass. A couple of people drop coins into his cup. Most do not. Fastidious, they walk around him and his piss. One band of youths laugh, pointing to the pools. Three armed soldiers on patrol in camouflage outfits look, just as they look everywhere, for signs of insurgency. It's a full year after the last Red Shirt protests boiled over, but the government is still in power, the soldiers are still here and Chai is still hungry. No one asks the beggar if he wants to be moved. The police won't move him, Chai knows; they have been paid.

Chai leaves his post to turn and stroll past the soldiers. He stops to check his pockets as though he's looking for something and watches as, oblivious to his presence, the patrol descends on the opposite side. He returns to his vantage point.

Looking down, he can see his partner, Dit, standing a little back from the street with his motorcycle. Beside Dit, under a road construction sign like a pup tent, a dog rests in the shade. The naked red ulcers all over its body look sore. Its muzzle, now healed, has been crushed and twisted to one side, maybe from too close an encounter with a car. That painfully contorted dog face turns and turns, strangely peaceful, observing passers-by with quiet interest.

Dit is pretending to work on his motorcycle. That boy knows what he's doing; he has been around. Dit was a Ranger. Up in Korat. And last May he made good money as a Red Shirt guard. Dit laughs quietly and says that's because he wore black, not red. Chai was there too, but he only wore red.

Chai likes Dit's high-top sneakers, and he feels ashamed of his own rubber thongs. Though he wonders if the high-tops aren't hot in this weather. Maybe he'll buy a pair after the job, when he has money. Below, the traffic stops for the red light, and the dog turns to watch as, loose-limbed, flip-flops slapping a quick tattoo on the metal, Chai comes down the steps to stand on the pavement. Dit looks over at him, his manner questioning. But Chai just waves and lights a cigarette, the Marlboro Dit gave him earlier. Chai catches a glimpse of himself in the tinted windows of a passing Toyota Crown. He likes the sunglasses. Counterfeit Polaroids. Same as the real ones, but cheap. He takes the glasses off and hangs them on the collar of his T-shirt. Right now, this afternoon, he wants the city unmediated by his Polaroids. Maybe it's the heat, but the colors are brighter today. Hotter and brighter. More real. Especially without the sunglasses. Even with the pollution and the car exhaust, everything is so clear. "CHEVY CHASE" reads his brand-new T-shirt. Chai doesn't know any English, but the vendor who sold him the shirt explained that a Chevy Chase is an American car. That's what he's going to buy one day, Chai tells himself, admiring the logo on his shirt front. A Chevy Chase. He wants to tell Dit. After they are finished.

The Toyota Crown moves on. Cars snarl and wheeze at the intersection, stop and start, an intermittent river of shiny waxed reds and yellows and blues. All the colors in the world. Splendid hues multiplied and complicated in chrome and glass. A big air-conditioned bus rolls by, painted up like a new-model iPhone, its giant screen a window on some world of happy people.

Last year this part of town was a sea of red. Red shirts, red headbands, red banners, red pickup trucks and, finally, red blood on the streets. Even Chai came out in his brother's red Singha beer T-shirt and his reddish motorcycle taxi driver's vest. He got money every day he showed up. Not a lot, but they were going to bring the government down, he was told. Then there would be much more money for everyone. The old prime minister would return, bringing back "democrazy" with him. Nai Yai—the Big Boss—was the richest man in Thailand, maybe in the world. So everything would be okay again, everyone said. Chai believed them and tries to now, tries to remember the days when everything was okay.

Air-con bus fares have gone up again. Everything is going up. How can a person live in this city, the way things are going? You sit on an ordinary bus, no air, and the bus gets stuck in traffic, not even a breeze. It's torture. Clouds of exhaust choking you. You haven't got to work yet and you're all screwed up, your clothes soaked with sweat. Chai got off the bus three stops early, not wanting to be seen, and he walked the rest of the way to the overpass to meet Dit. You need a car in this city. A motorcycle is faster, but then you're right down there in the worst of it. Coughing all the time. Chest tight. Eyes sore. Motorcycles aren't the same as cars. Chai knows he'll be nobody until he can sit in his own car with his air-conditioner blowing and some music on his stereo. A nice girl beside him. Then it won't matter how bad the traffic is.

The Mercedes-Benzes and BMWs and Honda Accords roll by. Lots of Mitsubishis and Toyotas and Peugeots and Isuzus. Volvos. One Jaguar. But no butterscotch Benz. Not yet. It's amazing, with what they cost, the number of Mercedes-Benzes on the streets. When Chai gets his car, he wants smoked-glass windows all around; it looks good. And it keeps the sun out. But then how will people be able to see the nice girl beside him? It will be better if people can see her. He stares hard at the side windows of a passing Volvo, seeing only shadowy presences that could be anybody. No, not anybody. Someone rich. "Mobile Class Members Club," proclaims a sticker on the back window of one car. Chai has heard how much a single beer, a small beer, costs in a club like that one. The job his brother Vajira has, he doesn't earn that much in a day. Vajira's wife, Daeng, she doesn't make that much in three days, renting out woven mats in the park so people can sit on the grass. At a place like the Mobile Class Members Club the girls are all beautiful and, somebody told Chai, their drinks cost even more than the beer. And you know how much you have to pay to take one of these chickens home for the night? It's unbelievable.

But they say the Red Shirts are coming out again. And this time there'll be no stopping them. No more double standards. Everybody will have money. Nice cars. Good whiskey. Dit says all these things will come true. It's democrazy that does it. And then he laughs, maybe because this makes him happy.

The light is turning, so Chai goes back up the steel stairway to his post.

This job today will buy him a few beers. Beautiful women, too, though not in the Mobile Class. A motorcycle, bigger than his brother's. And this is only the start. If he does good work this time, there will be more in the future. This is a big chance for him. He'll be able to buy a car. A Toyota. He'll drive his brother and his wife to Nonthaburi, to that restaurant by the river. And they will eat big grilled tiger prawns with sweet solid white meat. And cold, cold beer. Even a bottle of Black Label whiskey. Put it on a trolley with a bucket of ice and bottles of cola. The waiters will keep pouring it out, nobody's glass allowed to go dry; then he'll call for more Coke and ice. And when the first bottle of Black Label is gone, he'll send a waiter for another. He'll buy a Blu-ray DVD player, and the neighbors will come to sit downstairs, on the road outside the house, and watch the Muay Thai boxing. A big color set with a forty-two-inch screen. HD. He'll buy everybody Mekong whiskey and beer and fried duck and prawns. No. He should buy them Black Label too.

A young woman stops to drop some coins into the legless beggar's cup. A nice-looking woman in a nice dress. She's wearing a chunky gold-chain necklace, and Chai sees the look in the beggar's face as he thanks her. Had the beggar legs to stand on, he would stand to snatch the gold and run like the wind. The woman walks down the steps to the street and towards the intersection. Chai likes the way she moves.

Chai suddenly sags, struck with the gravity of it all. Cars and motorcycles, tuk-tuks and trucks roar and whine and growl, a snarling confusion of sound, a weight of color and movement and want and hate, killing in this heat. Chai hasn't eaten yet today. It's too hot. The heat weighs down, threatens to suffocate him. The cityscape shimmers for a moment and then holds still again, intense and hard-edged.

A brown Mercedes-Benz is approaching... It isn't the one. The man told him to watch for a butterscotch Benz, the same color as the foreign *khanom*, the candy he gave Chai to taste. Expensive candy. What the foreigners eat, but it doesn't taste so good. Chai likes Thai food. And with that thought he feels pangs of hunger. He feels faint, dizzy. A dull throb has started in his temples. The butterscotch Benz is a big one, he has been told. An SE class. Chai repeats the license plate number he was given, repeats it over and over like a mantra. He steps to the other side of the bridge, the beggar's side, and looks towards the intersection to see the changes.

The gigantic mall they burned last year has been rebuilt; it seems bigger than it was before, and more beautiful. Chai has been inside only once. It's like a temple, but far grander than any temple he has ever seen. Behind the mall and there, on the other corner, they are building more things—who knows what? Chai gazes all around the city horizon and shakes his head to clear the dizziness. The sky burns inside his head. A silent scream, the insect battle cries of building cranes draw together in one long plangent shriek across the hot blue sky, a shrill of anxiety only he can hear. From wherever you stand these days, alien stick-figure monsters loom on the skyline, a tangle of mindless, implacable builders. Destroyers. Sometimes—now—Chai hates this great suppurating city, swollen with people and cars swarming like maggots on a week-old corpse, multiplying like bacteria in a wound till the pressure of pus threatens to burst the tissues.

They kept Chai and his brother awake for ten months, erecting the high-rise condominium where the noodle shop, the best in the neighborhood, and the adjoining ice-house used to stand. They worked twelve-hour shifts around the clock, seven days a week. Nobody could sleep, but it wouldn't have done any good to complain to the police. They had been paid. Now things are quiet once more, but Chai will never be able to see the sun from the roof of their building again. And now the lane is always choked with cars and delivery trucks. But *mai pen rai*—it doesn't matter; soon they will have to move anyway. Another condo is going up and the whole row of old houses, the grocery and the barbershop have to go. Rents are so high these days, though; it's hard to say where they will move to.

Before they tore down the old wooden ice-house, Sombat the legless boy used to clatter around the neighborhood on his cart delivering baskets of crushed ice. After the ice-house went, the rattle and squeak grew less frequent, slower, somehow less cheerful. For months before he died, Sombat gradually faded away, sometimes sitting for hours on the street doing nothing, just looking, smiling a bit if you said hello.

Black-smoked windshields throw reflections of Chai back up at himself, phantom witnesses to his presence, watching and waiting there this day. And now the moment is moving surely towards him. It approaches with the stuttering river of cars, with the slow storm of color and sparkle in the hot, still air. Reds flare fierce as blood in the sun, blare lust and power. Blues dazzle and pine. Dark greens, cool greens; hot yellows and pinks. Glossy black class—power. The whole of it a hectic crawl, a babble of color, a confusion of grays, whites, maroons, browns, silver and gold, a vast hubbub of sorrow and anger and want and hate. And here it is—a big, long S-class. The butterscotch Benz is approaching, slick and sweet enough to eat. The inside lane, as well. That's good. And it isn't going to make the green light.

Chai clatters down the steps and swings onto the bike behind Dit even before the Benz has stopped, stuck behind a truck and two cars at the intersection. Dit moves the motorcycle out to draw alongside, Chai riding pillion. *Jai yen yen.* Cool, cool; be cool, now. Chai reaches inside the saddlebag.

They'll wait till the light turns yellow.

Chai waits and waits as Dit revs the throttle, looking to see the shadowy figures in the back seat of the Benz. Two people. And the driver in front. This is work, remember, Chai tells himself as the bike pulls ahead a little. Do it right. Keep cool. But his heart sings as he pulls the trigger again and again, the big pistol bucking in his hand as the smoked glass shatters and sags and caves in to reveal just another person, after all, vulnerable like the rest of us, his face dissolving in shock and then in blood. The only sound now, for Chai, is the bark of the 11mm automatic pistol, the only voice the gun, the only business the revelation of this soft, silly creature trying to hide behind his hands, behind his glasses as they, too, shatter and explode in hot red blood. With a quick look of alert intelligence, the dog hunches farther back under its shelter.

Chai puts on his sunglasses again. To cool things down; to give him distance. As they pull away, he can hear a woman screaming, maybe the one in the car. Dit angles the motorcycle through the jam of cars, scooting around a panel truck, behind a bus and then off through the intersection to lose them in the traffic. Chai never hears the mighty howl as the legless beggar rocks back and forth on the pavement, banging his cup till coins fly in all directions. "I am my iPhone," proclaims his T-shirt, white lettering on a red background.

Sunset comes quickly in the tropics. This day in April the whole city greets the dusk with gratitude. Back on the pedestrian overpass, two men come to take away the legless beggar. In Chai's part of town, bats dart against the sky, disappearing as the twilight dies and street lamps switch on. The street lights, the shop lights, the tail-lights of the evening traffic all lend a festive air to the city. Shabby, teeming streets throb to glad rhythms, to the honking wheeze of traffic, to the start and stop of buses, the cries of hawkers, the din of CD stalls. The pavements are crowded with vendors steaming, smoking, sizzling away side by side, blocking the pavement, the air rich with aromas of food, with the fragrance of jasmine and diesel.

Chai has finished his business for the day, and he has money. Now, finally, he's going to eat. He is hungry, hungry. The old noodle shop is gone. He and his new friends are going to try that new restaurant. It's air-conditioned and it has pretty waitresses in nice uniforms. Tonight he will drink beer.

In the morning he'll go to the temple and make merit. That will make his brother Vajira happy.

Collin Piprell

Collin Piprell is a Canadian writer and editor based in Bangkok.

He has also lived in England, where he did graduate work at Oxford, and in Kuwait, where he learned to sail, waterski, and make a credible red wine in plastic garbage bins. Before and after the Oxford and Kuwait years Collin was, among other things, a driller and stope leader on four mining and tunneling jobs in Ontario and Quebec.

Over the past years he has produced many articles on a wide variety of topics. He is also the author of four novels, a collection of occasional pieces, a diving guide to Thailand, another book on diving, and a book on Thailand's coral reefs. He has also co-authored a book on Thailand's national parks.

Official Website: http://www.collinpiprell.com.

Lightning Source UK Ltd.
Milton Keynes UK
UKOW031514121111

181960UK00008B/8/P